KINGDOM OF THE NORTHERN SUN

The Revolution Series

KINGDOM
OF THE
NORTHERN SUN

The Revolution Series

CLARA MARTIN

LUMINARE PRESS
WWW.LUMINAREPRESS.COM

Cover Art by JD&J
Cover Layout: Melissa K. Thomas

Luminare Press
442 Charnelton St.
Eugene, OR 97401
www.luminarepress.com

LCCN: 2019941768
ISBN: 978-1-64388-144-7

DEDICATION

*To my brother, Josiah, and
my mother, Beth*

ACKNOWLEDGEMENTS

*With many thanks to Brittany
Morgan, poet and writer (check her
out on Instagram at @blndechick23)
and
Michelle Malatek, amazing friend
Bergen Nelson, friend and editor
Maureen Rutkowski, amazing friend*

CHAPTER 1

‑‑‑‑‑‑‑‑◆‑‑‑‑‑‑‑‑

I WAS DREAMING, AGAIN. Somewhere I knew it; somewhere, I could feel my body struggling to wake up. But all I could focus on was the angry, warped face; the body lying across the pavement; the pain burning across my head. I screamed, bringing my hands to my face. I woke, then, feeling the imprint of my hands on my face, my pulse racing, the scream caught in my throat.

You'll never be alone, Sheldon whispered in my head. *We're here.*

Yes, Joe agreed. *We're here.*

"Go away," I rasped, raising my head gingerly. My muscles were cramped. I lifted my hand to my forehead again, half expecting to feel blood. There was nothing there. In my head, Joe sniggered. *You'll never be alone*, he murmured.

"Go away," I snapped. I glanced at my cell phone. It was two hours before I was supposed to wake, but I knew there'd be no more sleep tonight. Groaning, I swung myself out of bed. I might as well prepare for my interview

Later, I strode down the streets of Washington, DC, after nearly giving up my soul for parking. My resume crinkled as I readjusted my grip, trying to keep my sweaty palms from touching the expensive paper. This interview was the one—I could feel it.

The day was beautiful, and I tried to appreciate it as I walked down the street. This was a less congested part of Washington. While the areas closer to the Beltway were crowded with cars, there were more horse-drawn carriages to be seen here. They drove by slowly, coats of arms proudly displayed on the carriage doors, horses bedecked in their house colors. I looked at the stores as I passed, noting the names. Fine Alchemy. Siobhan's Finery for Ladies and Gentlemen. Divine Tastes, a small sweets shop. Each store was small and upscale, clearly catering to the politicians who swarmed Washington—and the fae nobles who ventured from their plantations in the South and the Midwest.

I stopped at a small, standalone red building. It was unmarred by store signs, the only mark on it a street address. I pulled out my iPhone and double-checked the confirmation email. Yes. This was McConnell Consultants, and I was right on time for my interview. Swallowing, I squared my shoulders and walked up to the door. When I turned the knob the door glowed blue for a moment, and I groaned. I tapped on the door instead, sighing. This was not the way I'd hoped my interview would start.

The door opened, and an older man, perhaps fifty or sixty, peered out. He had a hooked nose, a full head of grey hair, and somber brown eyes. "Ms. O'Donnell?" he asked.

"Yes, sir," I replied, smiling desperately.

He looked at me, head cocked to the side. "You can't open a simple door ward, Ms. O'Donnell?"

I sighed. "No, sir. I had an accident when I was in the US Army. Magic is completely inaccessible to me."

He raised his eyebrows, then nodded. "I'm sorry to hear it, Ms. O'Donnell. If you're hired, we will of course make allowances for that. Please, do come in." He opened the door wider and gestured.

"Thank you, sir." I stepped in and found myself in an opulently appointed waiting room. "We'll be in my office," the man said, leading me to one of four heavy oaken doors. "Please, sit."

I sat, looking around the office. The chair I was in was comfortable leather. A heavy oaken desk sat between us. A small globe filled with fae lights danced on the desk—it was being used to hold down several embossed leather folders.

"Ms. O'Donnell." The man took a seat behind his desk and folded his hands. "I am Mr. McConnell. If this interview proves fruitful, it would be my pleasure to hire you as an associate with McConnell Consultants." He paused. "Do you have your resume?"

I swallowed and handed it to him. He nodded once and glanced at it, turning the page.

"I see you were an officer in the US Army," he said. "What was your branch?"

"I was an ordnance officer, sir."

He frowned. "You say you cannot do magic, but I see you received a certificate from the Army's Basic Officer Leadership Course—does that not include basic tactical magic?"

"It does, sir. I had an accident about three years into my commission." I folded my hands together, desperately attempting to present a normal facade. "I have been unable to use magic since."

"I see." He looked at my resume again. "You do have a great deal of experience in leadership and teamwork. You were honorably discharged for medical reasons about six months ago. What have you done with your time?"

"Mostly interviewed for jobs, sir." I kept my hands folded tightly. I needed this job—the money the VA had awarded me for my injury was running out. I just desperately hoped he wouldn't inquire too closely about my six-month gap.

He smiled tightly. "So what attracts you to my company, Ms. O'Donnell?"

I took a deep breath. "I admire high-quality organizations and would like to think critically and use the skills I developed in the army," I replied.

"Let me explain, Ms. O'Donnell, that my company does work with fae. In fact, they're some of our major clients. Does that present a problem?"

"No, sir. It doesn't."

He gave another tight smile. "Well then. You certainly have an excellent resume, and these letters of recommendation are quite strong. I'll have to call them, of course, and I see one is overseas so I suppose I'll have to do a Sending—but shall we say you're provisionally hired?"

I barely stopped myself from whooping with joy. Finally—a job!

"I'm honored to accept, sir," I said quietly.

"Excellent," Mr. McConnell said, standing. "My secretary will contact you with the particulars."

I walked out into the waiting room, restraining my broad grin, and then stopped dead. A desperate face was peering through the window.

The face was a woman's, young, thoroughly beaten; both her eyes were black, and I could see scars around her neck. She held a baby, not more than a month old, wrapped in rags. When she saw me, she held the baby up and pointed to the door. Please, she mouthed.

In a single stride, I crossed to the door and opened it. The woman ran in, clutching the baby tightly to her.

"Please," she whispered. "Help me." She shivered and hunched over the baby as if to protect it.

"What's wrong? What do you need?"

"He can't find me," she whispered again. "Please. Hide me. He's almost here."

Quickly, I shoved her behind one of the sofas. "Stay down," I whispered. I looked to Mr. McConnell's office. I couldn't leave the woman, but I desperately hoped that this would not lose me my job on the day I got it.

The woman mewled, a wordless noise of anguish. "Quiet," I whispered frantically, cursing my inability to do magic. For what I suspected was coming, I would have felt better with a few combat spells at the ready.

Outside the window, I could see a fae carriage slow, then stop. This one was black, with a red coat of arms on the door—a screaming eagle, clutching a bleeding snake in its talons. The door opened. Two fae men sprang from the carriage.

They were both handsome, as fae are wont to be—tall, well-muscled, with an air of unshakeable confidence I could sense through the window. They wore black armor, embossed with the same seal as on the carriage—but one, I noted, feeling faint, had a crown above it.

A royal. This couldn't possibly get better.

The royal had black hair, black eyes, and swarthy skin. His eyes scanned the street, hands held in battle-magic position. Unerringly, he marched straight to the office. I bowed my head. I could feel the power of the Word he used to open the door from where I stood.

He stood framed in the door, eyes traveling dismissively over the office. "I am in search," he said, his voice a deep, silken tone that chilled me to my toes, "of a woman. A slave. Where is she?"

I cleared my throat, pulling my shoulders back. "There is no one here, my lord."

His eyes snapped to me, and his eyebrows lifted mockingly. "No one?" he asked, voice turning dry. He stepped through the door.

"There's definitely someone here," a voice behind him said. I glanced behind the royal and cursed myself. I'd completely forgotten about the second fae.

"Myself and my employer," I said curtly.

"It is difficult to distinguish between human life forces," the royal said. "You do, I admit, form a blob in my sensing magic. But no, my dear. The slave is here."

I crossed my arms. "You do not have permission to search this office."

The second fae laughed. "We don't need it. The slave has been missing for under a year. The sanctuary law does not apply." He snapped his fingers dismissively.

The royal was watching me, his eyebrows creased. "I am Faolain, prince of Northern Sun," he said abruptly. "Whom do I have the pleasure of addressing?"

That was unexpected. I drew myself taller, feeling as though my spine might snap from the rigidity. "I am Eileen O'Donnell." I caught myself before giving my rank. I no longer held that right.

Prince Faolain frowned, staring at me still more intensely. Suddenly, he crossed the room in a single stride and grasped my wrist.

It burned. By the Lady of the Lake did it burn. I breathed sharply through my nose, unwilling to scream. I felt heat rush through me, from head to toe; I felt it touch my heart and explode. Then suddenly, it seemed to withdraw, straight back into Prince Faolain. He released me slowly, then lifted his hand. It began to glow blue, and a lancet of fire appeared on his fingers.

"Witch," he whispered. The lancet began to grow, sparking ominously. "What did you do, human witch?"

"I did nothing," I snapped, quickly moving into fight stance. I wouldn't be able to fight him magically, but I could at least get in a good punch before he took me down.

Prince Faolain looked at me, eyes furious. The fae behind him stared at me, eyes wide. I lifted my hands to my face, hands spread, waiting, thanking the Lord above for my time spent in Muay Thai class.

The lancet sparked again and arched off his fingers, gathering strength as it drove toward me. I wove, feeling my muscles wake as the adrenaline flowed through me. Coming back up, I drove my fist straight at Prince Faolain's nose, then snapped a kick at his stomach. He folded forward with a grunt and rose, slowly, hand sparking again.

"Witch," he hissed, "I'll kill you for what you've done."

Not replying, I snapped another kick at him, then rushed in closer, aiming for his neck. Prince Faolain's hand rose again and the lancet rushed toward me; I leaned to the side, allowing it to pass harmlessly. I jumped, grabbing his neck; Prince Faolain roared in rage, bringing his hand up again as I drove his face down, straight into my knee.

"My lord!" The second fae sounded terrified. "Please, my lord—if you kill her, you'll die as well!"

I smirked. "First he's got to get in a shot," I taunted, using my leg to tumble him to the floor. I aimed a low kick at his stomach but missed, as a sparkling barrier rose up between us. Prince Faolain rose slowly, one arm cradling his stomach, eyes narrowed.

"You're on my list, witch," he said, voice now very cold and even. "I'll remember what you did to me." He pointed at me, and I felt a sharp pain on my shoulder. "You should've left well enough alone," he snapped.

I heard a door open behind me. "My lord!" Mr. McConnell sounded harassed. "My lord, are you all right?"

Prince Faolain's eyes swept to him. "I am fine," he said coldly. He gestured at me. "A small misunderstanding." He turned around, gesturing at the second fae. "Move," he snapped. Striding to the door, he raised his hand, pushing it outward in a sharp motion. The door flew open with a bang.

I turned around, eyeing the sofa. There was no noise. I looked at Mr. McConnell, sighing. "Sir," I said politely.

His face was red, his hands clenched. "Prince Faolain," he said coldly, "is one of our best clients. Whatever your personal differences, that performance was simply abominable. I'm afraid we won't be able to work together." His office door swung shut with a sharp click.

I sighed, clenching my hands together. That was the only interview I'd gotten after sending out my application to well over twenty businesses. If only I still had my last job.

Shaking aside the bitter lane my thoughts were going down, I walked to the sofa and peered behind. The woman was lying there, absolutely still, eyes wide. One hand was clamped over the baby's mouth, the other holding a knife at her own throat. She saw me and shivered, releasing the knife. It fell to the ground with a thump.

"I can't believe it," she whispered, staring at me. "Who are you?"

I extended my hand to her, pulling her up. The

baby sighed, moving in her grasp.

"My name is Eileen O'Donnell," I said shortly. "What's yours?"

"Sarah," she said slowly. "Sarah of Northern Sun." She shifted the baby. "This is Tara." She looked at me, eyes still wide, shaking slightly. "What now?"

"Now," I said, voice firm, "now we go somewhere safe. Let's go."

We walked out the destroyed door and down the street. Sarah twitched every time a carriage drove by, shrinking into my shadow.

"Walk slowly," I instructed her gently. "Stay with me. We're just two people going out on a walk." I looked at her and sighed. She was conspicuous, with her blackened eyes and scarred neck. I pulled off my coat and handed it to her. "Put this on."

Sarah quickly pulled it on, refusing to let go of the baby. I held my arms out in a silent offer; she shook her head, moving the baby from arm to arm as she pulled my coat on. The baby bore this silently. Once Sarah got the coat on, I pointed across the street. "That's my car," I said. "Let's go. We shouldn't linger here."

We got to my car and buckled in. I pulled out the keys and started it, praying. Fortunately it started up on the first try and I pulled out of the parking lot. I glanced over at Sarah. She had one hand, white-knuckled, on the handle on the ceiling. The other clutched Tara tightly.

"First time in a car?" I asked quietly. Sarah looked at me, eyes slightly wild.

"Yes," she said hesitantly. She paused. "Why did you help me?"

I grunted. "You were a slave?" I asked

"Yes. I was born on Northern Sun. When they sent me to the embassy here in Washington, I tried to escape."

I glanced at her again. "So you had no help?"

"No." Her grip on her baby tightened. I nodded, guiding the car through an intersection.

"When did you escape?" I asked gently.

Her eyes filled with tears. "Yesterday," she said, voice catching. "I've almost been caught three times. I can't use my magic—they'll find me."

I nodded. "Let's go get some coffee", I said, voice still gentle. "I know a safe place where we can go."

We drove in silence for forty-five minutes. I relaxed once I got to the Beltway—the fae rarely drove in cars, and the speed was too fast to allow for horse-drawn carriages. Once we got to Woodbridge, I slowed down, checking my mirrors again. No one had followed us. Just to be sure, I drove for twenty more minutes, taking random turns. Finally, I drove to the exit to Manassas.

"We're not being followed," I assured Sarah. She looked at me, eyes full of doubt.

"He has more than one way of following me," she whispered.

"There's a powerful blocking spell where we're going," I assured her. "You'll be safe there, for a while."

I took the Manassas exit, watching the trees flash by as we picked up speed. I was careful to drive only five above the speed limit—the last thing we needed was the police involved. After about ten minutes, I stopped at a light. When it turned green, I roared across two lanes of traffic and turned right, not bothering with my blinker. I smiled. That was always the best part of the trip. I looked at Sarah again; her grip had tightened on the handle.

We drove two blocks down a residential street. Finally, I stopped at a small house, set well back from the road. "We're here," I said, trying to make my voice sound confident. "Let's go."

Sarah looked at me again, eyes still wide. "Where are we?" she asked, voice soft.

"We're at the Unity Shelter," I told her, gesturing at the house. "It's a safe place for domestic violence victims."

Sarah frowned. "What's domestic violence?"

"It's when someone commits violence against someone else in the home," I explained, heart breaking. This was one of the worst parts of the business.

"I was a slave, Ms. O'Donnell," Sarah said, "Violence was normal."

"That, Sarah—and please, call me Eileen—is why you're here. Escaped slaves come here sometimes, if they manage to get in touch with us."

She frowned. "Us?"

"I used to be an advocate," I said shortly. "I'm not anymore." I gestured at the house. "Let's go."

We opened our car doors and got out. As we walked toward the house, I felt my heart rate pick up and my breath grow short. It'd been almost a month since I'd been here, and the familiarity of it made my heart ache.

I knocked on the door. A speaker turned on. "Password?"

"Corn," I said confidently.

The door cracked open. Arianna Burke stood on the other side, looking at me disapprovingly.

"Eileen, you shouldn't be here."

Arianna was an older woman, in her seventies, with white hair cropped close to her head. She walked with a cane, which she leaned on heavily.

"Arianna." I took a deep breath. "Please. Sarah needs help." I gestured at Sarah, who was looking nervously around her.

Arianna sighed.

"We shouldn't stand outside," I urged her.

"Come in," she said, grudgingly holding the door open. Sarah and I walked in, Sarah almost knocking over Arianna in her haste to get inside.

Arianna stopped me as I walked in, her hand on my arm. "Eileen, by rights I should call the police," she said, voice low. "You have no right to come here and use that password."

"Arianna, I found Sarah in DC literally running from the fae. What was I supposed to do? Let her be caught? Turn her out on the street?"

Arianna sighed again. "We'll talk later. Let's see what Sarah needs."

Arianna led us to her office. I looked around as we walked, feeling pain at the sight of the familiar hallways. A door opened slightly and a women peeked out. She gawked at me, and I stared back. It was Irene, one of the women I'd helped before I'd been fired. I felt my heart twinge. I smiled tentatively. She looked stonily back and shut the door with a bang.

Arianna stopped at her office, using a key to open the door. "Let's go in," she said gruffly. Sarah looked at me. I nodded encouragingly, and she took a deep breath and walked into the office.

It was a comfortable place but clearly showed the constraints of the budget; the chairs were stuffed but obviously from thrift stores, the desk listing on one leg. The file cabinet, also old and battered, was double locked. Three chairs were arranged in the room in a triangle formation, in front of the desk with its battered old computer. Arianna went to the desk and opened it, getting out some paperwork. "Intake paperwork," she explained to Sarah. "This is the only time we'll write your name down."

Sarah nodded, trembling. "He'll kill me if he finds me," she whispered.

Arianna nodded, businesslike. "We're in the business of hiding people," she explained. "Let's start talking, shall we?"

Sarah swallowed. "What's the price for staying here?"

"This is a free service. We don't charge. There are house rules to follow, but it's mostly about getting along with people." Arianna smiled. "Can you tell me your name, dear?"

Sarah swallowed again. "My name is Sarah of Northern Sun."

Arianna nodded and wrote it down. "When did you escape?"

Sarah burst into tears, burying her face in her baby's chest. "He'll kill me if he finds me," she sobbed. "He'll kill my baby, as a warning to the other slaves."

"Sarah," I murmured, "Can I put my hand on your shoulder?" Sarah shook her head, still sobbing. "No worries," I said. "This is a safe place. It's hidden. I made sure no one was following us. Is there anything else we can do, to make you feel better?"

Arianna cut her eyes to me. "Eileen is right," she said. "This is a safe place."

Sarah's sobs shuddered into gasps. "I'm sorry," she gasped.

"No need to apologize, Sarah," Arianna murmured. "Totally normal and understandable."

"I was born in Northern Sun," Sarah said, sounding choked. "I lived there all my life, until I went to the embassy. My mother died under the lash of the fae. I never knew my father. I just want a better life for Tara."

"We don't have to talk about anything you don't want to," Arianna said reassuringly. "I just need your name, age, age of any children, and a little bit about your trauma. You've given me everything except Tara's age."

"She's a month old," Sarah said, hugging her child tightly. The baby woke up and began to wail. Sarah rocked her comfortingly.

"Just a little about the rules, Sarah," Arianna said, walking to the file cabinet. "Don't tell anyone outside where we are. Don't go outside after nightfall. Don't eat anyone else's food. And, finally, no magic. Can you accept that?"

Sarah nodded, still rocking a crying Tara. Sarah's head was down and her shoulders bowed.

"Good. I'll show you to your room. Luckily, we have space." Arianna cut her eyes to me again. "You—stay here," she said sternly. "We need to talk." Arianna walked to Sarah and smiled. "Are you ready?"

Sarah looked at me nervously. I smiled reassuringly. "It'll be okay," I said. "Don't worry. It was good to meet you, Sarah."

Sarah swallowed again, the bruises around her eyes standing out even more after her tears. "Thank you—Eileen," she said awkwardly. "For what you did. At the office. I know it cost you."

I smiled again, trying to hide my pain. "What was I supposed to do? Just let you suffer? Feel better, Sarah."

Arianna led her out of the room, and I leaned back further into my chair. My life felt out of control. I had no job, no money, and no prospects. I'd gotten in a fight with a fae prince. I had no magic, and an illness to deal with as well. I'd been fired from my last job. What was I—a broken down, ill, useless woman—to do?

"Eileen." I glanced up with a start. Arianna had come back into the room. "Eileen," she said sternly, not bothering to sit, "You were fired from the Unity Shelter. I made an exception this time, but you can't do this again. Do you understand?"

I stood, heart heavy. "I understand, Arianna," I said, trying to keep my voice level. "But what else was I to do?"

"Next time," Arianna said harshly, "call the hotline." She held her office door open. "It's time for you to go."

I walked to the door, shoulders back, head high. We walked to the front door in silence. As she began to open the door, though, Arianna paused.

"Eileen," she said awkwardly, "Are you feeling—better?"

"Yes," I said, flatly.

"No more hallucinations?"

"I don't see what business of yours that is," I growled. I reached to the door and pushed it open, then walked out, not looking back.

CHAPTER 2

I DROVE BACK TO my home in silence. After my breakdown, I'd moved back in with my family; I lived with my brother, my mother, and my father. Fortunately no one was home when I pulled into the driveway. I needed to think.

I unlocked the door and went up to my room, kicking aside piles of clothes that lay on the floor. I pulled off my suit top and bottom and threw them on the back of my chair, then collapsed in my underwear onto my bed. I pulled my comforter over my head and began to cry.

Prince Faolain—Sarah's desperate face—the fight, for Sarah's life, and possibly my own. It was just too much. I couldn't handle it. I curled up into a ball.

You can't do it, one of the voices whispered. It was Joe, the voice that spoke to me the most often. I'd named him Joe after a captain I knew back in the army, who looked like a donkey. It helped, to name the voices. It made them less terrifying. *Just give up now.*

Yes, another voice chimed in, agreeing. I sighed. It was Sheldon, named after a coworker at the Unity Shelter. *Give up. Give up. Give up.*

My phone rang. I floundered my hand around, searching for it, the voices still thundering in the background. It was probably still in my suit pocket. I groaned. I didn't feel like moving. They could leave a voicemail. I curled back into my ball, cursing life.

"Eileen." A stern voice sounded from right next to me. I blinked and rolled over. A Sending cloud was next to my bed. It sparkled dark purple, a sign that I'd never received a Sending from this particular person before.

"Eileen, get up. Leave. You're in danger here, and you need to go." The voice paused. "Just drive. We'll find you."

I sat up, blinking. "Who are you?" I asked, wishing I had my old M4 rifle or Spellblaster.

The cloud sparkled again. "Eileen, get up. Leave. You're in danger here, and you need to go—"

"All right, all right," I muttered. It was a programmed Sending—probably no one was listening to my responses. I grabbed a pair of sweatpants and a T-shirt from my old unit that happened to be lying on the floor next to my bed. I smelled them, made a face, and threw them on anyway.

I paused. Was I sure this wasn't a hallucination? Usually I'd ask my brother or my mother, but neither of them were here. I sat back down.

"Go away," I told the Sending sternly. "Nobody's chasing me."

The Sending cloud sparkled again, a deep purple. No answer came.

I pulled the covers back over my head and swung my feet onto the bed. "Go. Away," I repeated. I grabbed the side of my bed, focusing on the hardness of the wood.

I must've fallen asleep, then, because I awoke to a pounding head and cramped muscles. I looked up—the Sending was gone.

Yawning, I stretched and sighed, pulling my cell phone out of my suit pocket. It was five o'clock—I'd slept for two hours. Checking my messages, I saw a missed call from an unknown number. There was no voicemail.

Probably spam. I swung my bathrobe on and went to the door, yawning again. It sounded like a good time for coffee.

I headed downstairs and looked around. No one was home yet. Grabbing the coffee canister from underneath the counter, I measured out the coffee and turned on the pot. Yawning again, I walked into the living room and turned on the news.

"—this is Channel 7 news. And today, a debate on the sanctuary law—is it really in our best interest? One congressman is trying to change it."

I looked up. Congressman Corey Hamilton was standing in his office, next to his desk, looking solemn.

"Sanctuary laws put us at odds with the fae," he declared, pounding his fist on the desk for emphasis. "We must protect our citizens, our people. That's why I'm fighting to have this law repealed. Sanctuary laws take money from law enforcement, from our taxpayers. And we don't even know if they work." He paused, pounding his fist again.

"Sanctuary laws currently state that any escaped fae slave may, after a year, be given citizenship in the United States. But why should we protect them? We need to protect ourselves—and the fae embassy has viciously protested this law since it was signed. How can we expect them to be our allies if we can't support them, as well?"

He opened his mouth to continue, but I snapped the television off, disgusted. I wished I had voted in the last election—he'd won by a very narrow margin.

My phone rang again. I glanced at it and sighed. It was another unknown number. I hit the ignore button, then turned the television back on. Maybe there was a *Forensic Magic* episode on.

My phone beeped with a text message. I picked it up. The text was from an unknown number as well.

"It'd be in your own best interest to answer your phone."

Frowning, I texted back.

"Who is this?"

Clara Martin

Almost as soon as I sent it, I got a reply.

"We could be your best friends. We want to be. We know what you did."

The phone rang, from that unknown number. I hesitated, then hit accept. I turned the television volume down and lifted it to my ear.

"Hello?"

"Hi, Eileen. I'm glad you finally answered. You ignored our phone calls—we were getting worried for a minute there." The voice on the other end was male, crisp and even.

"Why are you trying to talk to me? Who are you? Did you send the Sending?" I asked, clutching my phone. Scrambling to the side table, I picked up a pen and paper to take notes. How I wished I had a recording app on my phone, or could simply spell it to record!

"We didn't send a Sending, Eileen. We're trying to talk to you because you did something very brave today. And please, call me Garrett."

"I'm not sure what you're talking about, Garrett. I did nothing brave." I scribbled on the sheet, wondering if I should call Arianna and warn her about the attention.

"You saved a slave today, Eileen, both her and her child. She was as good as captured—and you stood between her and a very powerful fae. Prince Faolain should not be underestimated." Garrett sighed. "We're worried about you."

I hesitated. "I'm worried about me, too," I admitted. "I was so focused on getting Sarah out—but Prince Faolain threatened me."

"Unsurprising. It also makes it even more important that we move, quickly. Can you meet us tonight?"

"Where?"

"We're in Vienna. At 5060 Park Avenue. Should be about a forty-five-minute drive. Come at six—or should I say, Lieutenant O'Donnell, 1800." He laughed softly. "We did some research on you."

"Then you should know it's former Lieutenant O'Donnell," I snapped, pressing the pen hard against the paper.

"I don't think you every truly leave it behind, Eileen—and that's coming from 'former' Sergeant First Class Garrett Pine." Garrett laughed again. "There. A detail for a detail. You'll learn more about us tonight at six. Till then." The call ended.

I frowned. Garrett Pine had found my cell phone number. What if Prince Faolain did, as well? I glanced outside. Aside from the pine trees, there was nothing there.

What could I do? I felt a chill run down my spine. It was nothing, I told myself firmly. Prince Faolain wouldn't act so quickly—not while he was licking his wounds. I glanced at the phone screen. It was 5:15. If I left now, I'd make it exactly on time.

First, though, I pulled up Messenger and texted my mother.

"Got in a fight with a fae over a slave. I'm fine, nobody hurt, but going to meet some people about it. 5060 Park Dr. Vienna. Guy by the name of Garrett Pine."

Pocketing my phone, I headed out the door, snagging my keys and my purse. As I got in my car, I heard my phone buzz.

"What time will you be back? Do you want backup?"

I texted back, "Probably no later than nine. Will text if later. And no backup ... I'll just tell them I told you where I was going, lol."

With that, I pulled out of the driveway and sped down the street.

It took exactly forty-five minutes to make it to Park Avenue. I pulled up outside a small building, studying it. It was in the commercial part of Vienna and had the appearance of a refurbished store. Just like the Unity Shelter, it was set back from the street. At least there was a lot of parking. I pulled in and parked the car, jumping out and grabbing my keys and pepper spray from the glove box. Quickly, I walked to the door and tried to open it. A familiar blue glow shone around it. With a sigh, I knocked.

The door swung open. "Ah, Eileen O'Donnell," the man on the other side said. "Garrett Pine." He held out his hand, and I gave it a firm shake.

Garrett Pine, former Sergeant First Class in the United States Army, was at least forty. His hair was buzzed short to his scalp. His black skin shone in the light. He was easily six foot five, and muscled. I noticed the tattoo on his arm—the Ranger insignia. I hid a wince. As a Ranger, he'd be expertly trained in warfare, hand-to-hand combat, and battle magic. I wondered what kind of organization this was.

"Come in, please," he said, gesturing. I stepped in, looking about. The entrance hall was small and dark, lit by only one small fae light. The hallway led to a single door, glowing ominously blue.

Garrett led me to the door and, with a glance at me, leaned in close and whispered a word. The door smoothly creaked open. He waved me inside again, smiling. "Welcome, Eileen. This is the Northern Virginia Rescue Association."

I'd heard of them in the news—they frequently launched rescue attempts deep into fae-held territory. They were just this side of legal because of it. The NVRA was reputed to be well funded and well-staffed, certainly no collection of amateurs.

"So this is Ms. O'Donnell," a woman's voice said as I walked through the door. A small woman, gray hair caught up in a bun at the back of her head, came up and shook my hand. She smiled sympathetically. "I'm Helena. I see the damage, Eileen. I'm sorry for the trauma you went through."

I blinked. "How do you—" I asked suspiciously.

"I'm the local healer. My Sight shows me wounds. I see both the brain damage and the sickness. I'm sorry." She released my hand.

"That's extremely personal," I snapped.

"Don't worry, Eileen. I won't tell anyone here. I don't believe your medical condition makes you a danger to us. I just wanted you to know you have a friend in me." She nodded once, and turned back to sit.

The room was large and windowless, with maps hanging about the walls and a large table dominating the middle of the room. I recognized maps for Shenandoah, Northern Sun, Western Wind, and the Kingdom of Texas.

"Some of our areas of operation," Garrett said, coming up behind me. "The rebels in the Kingdom of Texas, in particular, are very active." He snorted. "They still hold a grudge for the Alamo." He waved his hand at the table. "Please, take a seat."

I sat, looking around. Helena sat next to me, and Garrett across from me. He smiled, bracing his hands on the table.

"Think of this as a pre-membership interview, Eileen. We want you to join us. We've looked up your history. You've been an advocate. You've served in the army. You had a proud track record in the army, as well, until your accident. Then today's performance? You're everything he want." His eyes sparkled. "But we need to make sure it's a good fit, for both of us."

I nodded. "I know you organize rescue missions into fae territory," I said slowly. "I don't know much more than that."

"We do. Technically, everyone we rescue is outside the estate they're running from already—it's a legal grey area. We're not allowed to set foot on the estate itself, but nobody said anything about the boundary area." Garrett laughed. "Then we spirit them back to human lands."

"How do you keep them safe until the sanctuary law kicks in?" I asked.

"We have safe houses we keep them in." He smiled. "Now, that's enough about us, Eileen. I'm curious about you. Your discharge document said you'd received some sort of injury."

I nodded slowly. "I did." I lifted my hand, looking at it. "I'm no longer able to use magic because of it."

Garrett nodded. "Problem for an officer. The officer corps uses magic for everything." I nodded again. "So tell me, Eileen. How did the injury occur? You were never deployed to Afghanistan, Iraq, or the Northern Wild."

I sighed. "I intervened in a fight. Caught a blow to the head. It probably would've been fine if I'd gone to the medic first thing, but I didn't. I shrugged it off."

Garrett looked at me sympathetically. "Probably not the best thing you could've done."

"No, it wasn't. I gradually lost the ability to use magic over the next week. Got blinding headaches. Fainted a few times. By the time I did go the medic, it was too late. They gave me an MMRI scan. The physical side showed the brain damage, right in the prefrontal cortex controlling magic use. The magical side showed that my magical aura had changed completely ... it's cut off from my body, now. The web is still there; I just can't use it."

"Hmm." Garrett eyed me. "Now tell me, Eileen. We talked to your old boss at the Unity Shelter. She mentioned something about hallucinations. Can you tell us about those?"

I sighed again. That was probably why I'd only gotten one job interview. "I started hallucinating at my old job. I was convinced someone was following me. It got pretty out of hand." I paused. "Eventually, my mother had me committed to a mental hospital. I've been on an antipsychotic regimen ever since."

I looked at Helena. She was looking at me sympathetically. "You're up and functioning now," she pointed out. "It looks like the antipsychotics work."

I nodded. "I take them every night."

"What was your official diagnosis?" Garrett cut in, his voice rumbling.

"Paranoid schizophrenia," I said heavily. "I still battle the paranoia sometimes."

He nodded. "Not a bad thing in our line of work," he remarked. "Is it related to the brain damage?"

I shrugged. "Nobody knows. Paranoid schizophrenia is usually genetic, but nobody in my family has it. The Department of Veterans Affairs is reviewing my case now ... I applied for disability."

Garrett nodded. "Be prepared to wait a few years. The VA is very, very slow." He smiled. "As Helena says, it looks like you're functioning pretty well to me."

"I try." I shrugged.

He slapped the table. "As far as I'm concerned, Eileen, you're in. Also—I understand you don't have a job?"

I nodded slowly. "I got one, then I got fired after my fight with Prince Faolain."

"The Northern Virginia Rescue Association would like to offer you a job as assistant program director. We don't pay much—about $1,500 a month—but it's more than you make now." He held out his hand. "Do we have a deal?"

I grasped it. "Yes. Yes we do. When do I start?"

Garrett smiled. "Right now. We have a rescue mission ongoing right now." He gestured at the door at the back of the room. "You ready?"

I took a deep breath. "Ready," I said.

"Let's go, then." He stood and walked to the door. He whispered another word and the door sprang open.

"You'll get your own passcode," he explained, holding open the door as I walked through.

The room I entered was also lined with maps, had several computers with people behind them, and had a Sending station. There was a long table in the center of the room. It reminded me of the War Room back at my old station's brigade.

"All right, everyone," Garrett said, clapping his hands. "This is Eileen. She's our newest member, and the assistant program director." He winked at me. "That"—he waved a hand at a man sitting behind a computer, intently monitoring an interactive map—"is Phillip Lafarge, another new member. And this"—he pointed at a woman seated at a second computer—"is Anna Tran, our program director and your new boss."

"Hey, Eileen," Anna said distractedly, still staring at the computer. "You're former army, right? You know anything about BFT?"

"Blue Force Tracker," I said. "We used a system at our last field training. It uses a combination of satellite and magic to track units in the field."

"Good. This is a modified BFT. We're good, but we don't have access to secure satellites, so we just track with magic and radio." She waved at Phillip. "Phillip over there has the BFT up, and I"—she held up a small handheld radio—"am monitoring radio traffic. We'd like to have a SINCGARS radio but we don't have the money."

"That's a short-distance radio," I said, puzzled. "Where's the rescue mission?"

Anna winked at me. "It is a short-distance radio ... except it isn't. I've magically extended its reach.

It's one of my gifts. Like you, I'm former army, but I was Signal Corps." She smiled. "They taught me a few useful tricks."

"So where's the rescue mission?"

She pointed to Phillip. "Go take a look at the BFT and see if you recognize the cartography."

I walked to Phillip and peered over his shoulder. Five dots, three labeled "NVRA" and two labeled "SOR," moved slowly across the map. The map was topographical, the lines on it representing hills, valleys, and ravines. I pointed to the line the five dots were headed down.

"They're on a mountain," I said, "following the ridge." I traced it on the screen with my finger. "It looks like they're in Shenandoah."

Phillip laughed. "Right on, Eileen," he said. "They've got a good head start over the hunters. This team is fire." He wiggled his fingers. "Two former Rangers and a Green Beret," he said by way of explanation. "The former military always seem to find their way here."

I took a good long look at him. Phillip was also tall, well-muscled, and clean-cut. His blonde hair was growing out of a buzz cut. I saw that he had a full sleeve of tribal tattoos up and down his arm.

"Army?" I hazarded a guess.

"Please. Better than that," he laughed. "Marine Corps." He cut a glance at me. "I thought I heard that you were army. Ever deploy?"

"No," I said shortly. "I was slated to when my injury occurred."

"Yeah, I heard about that, too," Phillip said, eyes going back to his screen. "No magic, huh? Sucks."

"It does," I agreed.

"Eileen," Anna called, "come over here and help with the radio."

I went over to Anna. Anna was shorter, five foot one but muscled. She gave the impression of a short, solid bundle of C-4—ready to explode with ferocity and energy. Her black hair was pulled back in a tight bun. She smiled distractedly. "They're about to call in," she explained. "I want you to be here to hear it."

I nodded, standing next to her chair. The radio spat.

"Charlie Tango to Base, break. Nine-line follows, break." There was a pause.

"Location. Grid coordinates 47891014 89891014. Break. Radio frequency. No change. Break. Two Alpha. Alpha. Two Bravo. Papa. Delta. Two Delta. Over."

"Base to Charlie Tango. Good copy." Anna leaned over and punched something into her computer. "Medevac en route. ETA five minutes. Out." Anna broke contact and leaned back. "So, catch all that?"

I nodded distractedly. "They needed a patient evacuation. They gave map grid coordinates. They'll be on this radio frequency. There're two patients, both urgent care. No special equipment required. Both patients are ambulatory. There are possible enemy troops in area, no method of marking the pickup spot, both patients are non-US civilians, and there's no nuclear, biological, chemical, or magical contamination."

"Excellent." Anna leaned back and crossed her arms. "We had medical personnel waiting at one of our safe houses," she explained. "They're en route to the meet-up spot now." She paused. "I'm a little worried about the enemy troops," she murmured. "We've been tracking the hunters the fae dispatched and they're nowhere near the area. I wonder what Talbot saw."

"Talbot?"

"Charles Talbot, the team leader. Former Ranger. Served for ten years then got out." She smiled. "I told you most of our members were former military."

"Except Jeanette," Phillip interjected. "And Helena. And Ross. And Rima—"

"Yes, yes." Anna waved her hand distractedly. "We bring in all kinds."

"So now what?" I asked.

Anna laughed. "We wait until the team makes contact from the safe house ... and then the relief shift comes in. And you're back here tomorrow, nine o'clock, to start your new duties."

I smiled and checked my watch. Eight thirty. "I need to text my mom," I said apologetically. "I told her where I was going and that I'd be back by nine."

She laughed again. "Didn't quite trust us, huh? Understandable. Go ahead and text her. Just no pictures."

I nodded, texting away. I put away my phone and looked up. Garrett was scrutinizing me.

"What time do you take your meds?" he asked abruptly.

I sighed. "Nine thirty, usually. I have them with me." I reached into my bag and pulled out a small bottle, tossing it to him. Garrett scrutinized it.

"Clozaril," he murmured. "Heavy-duty stuff." He tossed it back.

"Is there going to be a problem?" I asked sharply.

"None at all, as long as you stay on your meds," he said warningly.

"It's not something I mess around with," I snapped, stowing the medication back in my bag.

"Hey, no need to get defensive," Garrett said, holding up his hands. "You just have two serious disabilities. You're working around them. I can see that. But you gotta have your meds to function."

"I won't let you down," I promised, throat tight.

"I know," he said with a smile. "You're gonna do awesome, Eileen." He pointed to the table. "Have a seat. Now we wait."

Two minutes later, the radio cracked.

"Charlie Tango to Base, over."

Anna pressed the radio key. "Base to Charlie Tango, I read you."

"Sitrep follows, over." The radio cracked again. "8 November, 2100, break. Team 3, break. Present location, Safe House Charlie, break. Activity—securing rescues, break. Effective—ready to roll, break. Situation disposition—no change, over."

"Base to Charlie Tango, good copy. Out." Amy leaned back with a sigh. "So, what did you get?" she asked me.

"Well, they used the standard format for a commander's report. I'm assuming that's standard operating procedure. They sent the date and time, their unit name, their present location, what they were doing, whether they are combat effective or not, and if there were any changes to major combatant and support force locations."

Anna smiled. "You haven't lost it," she said, praising me. "Good work. I'll let you shadow me for the next few missions, and then you'll be able to take over and run one yourself."

I smiled back. "Awesome! How many missions do you run?"

"Depends on the season. These next two will probably be the last for the winter—we don't really do anything December through February. It snows pretty heavily in Western Wind and Northern Sun and makes tracking much easier and progress slow." "We do more in the summer months—maybe one a week." She sighed. "We usually only get one or two out at a time, but it does add up."

"How do you get the money?"

Anna winked. "You're not cleared for that yet, Eileen," she said with a smile. "We aren't rich, but we're not going to go broke anytime soon, either. Maybe next we'll get a SINCGARS." She hefted the small radio. "This takes a lot of magic to use."

I sighed. "I may not be able to use it, then," I said apologetically. "I can't use magic."

Anna blinked. "I had heard that," she said slowly, "but I hadn't realized you couldn't use it at all. Fine. We'll have you on the BFT, and Phillip here" —she waved at him— "can take radio duty."

"Awesome," Phillip said, looking up from his computer screen. "This gets old after a while." He winked at me.

"So when does the team come back?" I asked, leaning back from Phillip.

"They'll spend the night in the safe house and come back tomorrow," Phillip said, looking back to his computer. "We monitor the map to see if any of our friendly trackers pop up—the next shift should be here any moment."

With that, the door opened. Two women walked in.

"Evening, folks," one of the woman said, smiling. She looked at me. "New person? Nice to meet you. I'm Rima." She shook my hand. Rima was midsize, curvy, with a waterfall of brown hair falling down her back. She hitched it behind her ears, her bell earrings dancing.

"And I," the other woman said, coming from behind her, "Am Lia. Short for Thalia. Nice to meet you." Lia could've been Rima's twin, except her hair was a brilliant red.

"No canoodling in the War Room," Garrett warned. "I don't know why they put you two on shift together."

"Because we work so well together?" Lia asked innocently, twirling a piece of red hair around her finger.

"I'm not going to start making out with my wife in the middle of a shift, Garrett," Rima added, rolling her eyes. "Lighten up. You're not in the army anymore."

Garrett frowned. "We need to take this seriously," he said sternly.

"And we do," Rima said, waving her hand. "Why don't you go get some sleep?"

Anna pushed the chair back, levering herself to her feet. "I'm gone," she announced. She looked at me. "Eileen, you go too. You're going to need to be ready to go, bright and early."

I nodded, stretching. I could feel the knots of tension in my spine. It'd been a long day.

"Am I—safe to go home?" I asked, remembering what the Sending had said.

Garrett laughed. "By now, Faolain's spies have told him where you are," he said, eyes shining. "He doesn't want to pick an outright fight with us—he knows we've got your back. Go home. Get some rest."

Phillip stood up as well, saluting me. "I heard the story of what you did, Eileen," he said gravely. "That took balls. Good for you." He walked past me, opening the door and heading out.

"Seriously, Eileen," Amy said, walking to the door as well, "go home. Faolain won't bother you." She smiled at me. "I'll see you tomorrow."

I nodded waving. I checked the time—nine thirty. I grabbed the Clozaril from my purse and swallowed it.

"Good night," I said to Garrett, who was scrutinizing me. I walked out the door, as well.

What a day.

CHAPTER 3

⸺◆⸺

I WOKE UP THE next morning feeling refreshed. My sleep had been peaceful, unmarred by bad dreams or insomnia. I smiled, stretching, and headed downstairs to the kitchen.

"Good morning, Mom," I said, kissing my mother on the cheek. "How are you?"

She eyed me sharply. "What happened yesterday?"

I sighed. My mother was shorter than me, five foot five, with wispy brown hair and a petite build. Despite the petiteness, she was a firecracker when she wanted to be—a testimony to her past as a police officer. I often teased her about how she'd gone from law enforcement to teaching. "Is it really that different?" I would ask, jokingly.

"I intervened in a fight, Mom," I said, shrugging. "There was a fae slave. A fae came in and tried to retrieve her." I smiled in pride. "I think I broke his nose."

My mother sighed. "You have to be careful, Eileen. He won't forget that."

"I know, Mom. But I have a new job. Assistant program director, at the Northern Virginia Rescue Association."

My mother narrowed her eyes thoughtfully. "That's a good organization," she said. She turned and gave me a hug. "Keep going to Muay Thai, and carry your pepper spray. Get something for your car. Maybe you should think about buying a gun."

"I can't buy a gun, Mom. I was involuntarily committed to a mental hospital," I said with a sigh.

She frowned. "You need to apply to the court to get your privilege back," she said. "This is nothing to mess around with, Eileen."

I nodded. "I know, Mom. I'll be careful."

She nodded back, lips tight. "I know you will be." She picked up her coffee thermos. "I need to get to school. I'll see you when you get home." She smiled at me. "Congratulations on the new job."

I smiled. "Thank you," I said. I went back upstairs and changed out of my pajamas, picking out a black pair of pants and turquoise sweater for my first day of work. It let me move but looked casually professional. That seemed to be the vibe at the NVRA.

I drove to work, listening to the news. There was more debate about repealing the sanctuary law. "What is happening to us," the commentator asked despairingly, "that we would refuse to shelter our own kind against the fae, power-grubbing and cruel as they are?"

I nodded in agreement as I pulled into the parking lot, getting out and swinging my purse across my body. I made it to the door and paused. The door ward was still shining.

I knocked, and a few moments later a woman opened the door. "Yes?" she asked, blinking at me.

I smiled uncertainly. "My name is Eileen O'Donnell—I'm starting work today as assistant program director."

She frowned. "I didn't know anyone had been hired," she said querulously. She gazed at me, eyes sparking. I braced myself, recognizing a Truth spell. "What are you doing here?" she hissed.

I felt the Truth spell take hold. Truth spells could be fought, but only with a combination of willpower and mental focus. I gazed at her, staring at her nose, and resisted. I felt myself sputter as the words began to bubble to the surface.

"Jenny!" Garrett came up behind her. "What are you doing?"

Jenny frowned again. I felt the Truth spell break. "She came to the door, saying she was the new assistant program director."

"She is, Jenny." Garrett gently pushed her aside. "We'll talk about your use of Truth spells later. Eileen, come in."

I walked past Jenny, who was staring at me, and smiled at Garrett. I could feel a headache beginning to throb in my left temple. "Good morning, Garrett,"

I said politely. "Can I get a password to the door?"

"There's no password to the door ward—you have to use magic to open it. It's how we recognize people." He sighed. "We'll have to build in a loophole for you." He waved his hand into the first room. "As for the door to the conference room and the door to the War Room, absolutely. We'll get it set up this morning." Garrett guided me down the hall and leaned into the conference room door, murmuring a word. The door sprang open. "I can tell you're former army," he remarked. "You're fifteen minutes early."

"On time is late," I quoted.

He grunted, sitting heavily at the table. "We're just waiting for Anna," he said. "She'll be late. She always is."

The door behind us swung open. "Good morning, Garrett," a jovial voice boomed in. "Strike Team 3 is home." A man walked in the door, followed by two others.

The man in the lead was tall and bulky, built like a football player. He had long, shaggy black hair and a beard. I swallowed a gasp. I could feel the magic crackling off him—a veritable bonfire of power. His gaze swept to me.

"And who," he murmured, "is this?" He stared at me. I stared back, holding his eyes.

"This is Eileen O' Donnell," Garrett said, waving at me. "You missed the dramatics while you were out vacationing in Winter Wind."

The man laughed, showing clean, white teeth. "Oh?" he asked, smiling. "What happened?"

Garrett grunted again. "Why don't you tell him, Eileen," he said.

"I got in a fight," I said shortly.

The man laughed again. "Must've been some fight," he remarked. His eyes trailed over my face.

I shrugged. "It was interesting."

"Eileen is our new assistant program director," Garrett said. "Eileen, this is Charlie Tango, who you heard over the radio last night. Also known as Charles Talbot."

I stood and walked over, extending my hand. "Pleasure," I said.

Charles took my hand and stood there, staring into my eyes. "Christ," he said, releasing my hand. "You've been through the wars, haven't you?"

I shrugged again. "I never deployed," I said, voice tight.

He stared at me. "How did you—"

"That's enough," Garrett said, standing. "Come back here, you three. We need to debrief." All three men filed past me, shooting curious looks in my direction. Anna arrived in their wake.

"I'm sorry, Garrett," she said, voice distracted. "My car wouldn't start."

He grunted. "Seems like a recurring problem, Anna," he said, voice skeptical. "Why don't we get started, and after you're done, you can call a mechanic about your car. Like you should've done last time." He stared at her, raising an eyebrow. She seemed to shrink.

"No problem," she said dejectedly. She sat down in one of the chairs. "We'll take about five minutes here, and then go back to debrief," Anna told me. "First, here's your password." She pulled out a sheet of paper from her briefcase and passed it to me. "It's bloodlocked," she added.

I nodded. "Do you have safety pin?" I asked.

She passed me one, and I pricked my finger on the pin and smeared the blood drop on the sheet. Words began to sparkle on the paper. *Unicorn*, I read. Then, *Griffin*.

"The first one is the passcode to the conference room," Anna explained. "The second, to the War Room. Don't repeat them where anyone can hear them, and—" she pointed at the paper. It crackled in a sudden burst of flame, burning up before my eyes. "That's that," she said in satisfaction. "Any questions?"

"No," I said, shaking my head.

"Excellent," Anna replied, standing and gathering her briefcase. Garrett stood, as well. "Let's go to the debriefing, then." She led the way to the War Room door, whispering the word and closing the door behind her.

Garrett looked at me. "Standard precaution," he explained. "Some of the fae can shape-shift. We had one shifter try to get into the War Room, but he was caught when he didn't know the passcode." He whispered to the door, opened it, and shut it in my face.

I swallowed, leaning in close. "Griffin," I murmured. The door opened once more. I walked in, closing it gently behind me.

The three men from Strike Team 3 were sitting around the War Room table. Charles had a piece of paper in front of him and was rapidly scanning it. One of the other men had an open newspaper. The third man stared into space, looking sleepy. Anna sat at the head of the table and gestured for me to join her. I sat to her right. Garrett took the opposite side.

"Welcome," she said, "and good job, Strike Team 3. Before we begin, I want to introduce the new assistant program director"—she pointed at me—"Eileen O'Donnell."

I nodded to the table, smiling. The men nodded back.

"Good to be home," Charles said, smiling back at me.

The other two men exchanged looks. "You've met Charles," one of them volunteered. He was Asian, tall and rangy. "I'm Vu. Vu Mariner." I nodded at him.

"Jim," the third said laconically. He blinked, still sleepy. "Jim O'Rourke." He was shorter, also rangy, with brown hair that hung to his waist.

"Pleasure," I told all three. I leaned back in my chair.

"Now," Anna said. "Let's hear it."

Charles nodded. "We infiltrated the boundary of Western Wind," he said, pushing a map to the center of the table. There was a red X marked at one point. "We met up with the retrieval target and her child. We escorted them to the safe house in Shenandoah." He paused.

"We were pursued by three hunters, all from Western Wind. All second-rate. The Queen of Western Wind must not have placed much value on this particular slave. They were three days behind us, and we had them running in circles. We reached the safe house without incident."

Anna nodded. "We tracked them with the BFT," she said. "They seemed to have no idea how to track."

Charles nodded back. "The retrieval target and her child were safe and sound when we left." He pulled the map back. "The mission planned for next week, to Northern Sun, should be more interesting."

Anna smiled. "Anything to add, gentlemen?" she asked the other two men. They both shook their heads. "Excellent," she said. "You're dismissed and off duty for the next two days. Go recover."

Garrett cleared his throat. "And clean your gear," he added. "I can smell it from here." He frowned at Jim. Jim smirked.

Charles laughed. "Yes, First Sergeant," he said, grinning. He stood. "All right, you two. Go," he told the other two men. They stood and filed out of the room.

Charles looked at me. "So, new assistant program director," he said, voice taunting, "Any thoughts?"

I raised my eyebrows. "Seems like you did pretty well," I said lightly.

"We did." He dropped into the seat next to me. "My team is the best team." He studied me for a moment, frowning slightly.

"I see the damage," he said slowly, "but I don't understand how it could've occurred. That must've been a hard blow."

"Do you all know nothing of privacy?" I asked, irritated.

"No," he said, laughing slightly. "I'm used to assessing the health and combat capabilities of everyone I meet. You look fit for the office, not the field."

I glared at him. "I'm more than capable," I said tightly.

"Never said you weren't," he said lightly. "But I wouldn't take you on a mission, that's for sure." He eyed me. "Want to get coffee? I'll pay," he said abruptly.

I laughed. "Thanks, no, I'm fine." I leaned back in my chair. "I'm here. In the office. Being capable."

His mouth compressed into a thin line. "Your loss," he said, rising. "Nice to meet you, Eileen. I'm sure that I'll see you around." He gave me a shallow bow, his eyes dancing. I stared at him, unimpressed. "Garrett. Anna," he said, nodding to each in turn. He strode out of the room, banging the door shut behind him.

Anna sighed. "Of course he did," she muttered. "That man is a hound dog." She glanced at me. "Charles Talbot hits on every woman he meets," she added, "and most of them accept when he asks them to coffee." She laughed. "I think you're the first to have turned him down in almost two years."

I grunted. "I have better things to do with my time," I muttered.

"Of course you do," Anna said lightly, "Especially now that you're assistant program director." She pulled another sheet out of her briefcase. "We have two more missions in November. Let's start planning."

"Mission planning?" Phillip walked in, smiling. "I'm right on time, then."

"Phillip," I said slowly, "What exactly do you do?"

He smiled at me. "I don't have to attend the debriefs," he said, answering my unspoken question. "I'm a communications specialist." He grabbed the chair Charles had just vacated, stretching out. "Let's go, then."

Anna pulled a map from her briefcase, smoothing it out. "This," she said, gesturing at it, "is a map of Northern Sun." I looked at it. There was frighteningly little detail.

"We've never been inside the estate," she said, glancing at me, "and there's little detail to go off of, except what we gather on missions." She pointed at the boundary of the estate. It was more detailed, cartographic representations of ravines stretching out parallel to each other. "Satellite doesn't work over this particular estate. The King, Lugh, is very powerful and able to block it. You've met his son, Faolain," she continued, glancing at me. "Faolain does most of Lugh's dirty work. This is one of the most difficult estates to infiltrate. Strike Team 3 will be going out next week to meet two slaves and bring them back. This is a longer trek than Western Wind. The closest safe house is in Vermont." She pulled out another map, this time of the continental United States. The Northern Wild, Northern Sun, Western Wind, and the Kingdom of Texas were marked out in an ominous red. The thirteen states and California were colored a friendly blue. Anna pointed at Vermont. "We need to get a medic team to the safe house there without Faolain noticing—he has eyes on our building and operation," she explained to me. "This safe house isn't often used, so we can't station a medic team there permanently ... and we can't let him know that there's a mission planned. Any movement to Vermont could potentially alert him and make the team's mission more perilous." She sighed, leaning back. "Ideas?"

"Isn't there a football game up in Delaware, at one of the universities there?" I asked thoughtfully.

"There is." Anna tapped her pen on the table. "Are you thinking send the medic team to the football game?"

"Send a lot of people to the football game," I said. "Just stick the medic team in there with all the folks heading there." I pointed at the map. "They can head to the safe house after the football game. They'll just have to be careful not to be spotted en route."

"It is a less direct route than straight from here to Vermont," Phillip said. And it's less likely Faolain will pay attention to a large group of people heading out for entertainment."

Anna nodded briskly. "Garrett, thoughts?"

Garrett leaned back in his chair. "Makes sense to me," he said laconically. "We only need four people—two medics and two EMTs." He glanced at me. "We just need to find a large group of people for the football game."

"My brother goes to George Mason," I said slowly. "He told me that one of the clubs there is preparing a spirit trip."

Garrett raised his eyebrows. "Now how," he said skeptically, "are we going to get four people in with a bunch of college kids?"

"I could ask my brother if a group could travel along," I said. "He's the secretary of the club." I paused. "The only problem is that it's the Society of Law, and it would be a lot less conspicuous if the four people chosen could talk law."

Anna laughed. "We'll tell them to brush up," she said. "Okay. Can you call your brother?" She gestured at me.

I nodded, pulling out my phone. "He shouldn't be in class," I said, checking the time. I brought up my contact list and pressed the contact labelled "Thing 2." He answered on the second ring.

"What's up?"

"Hey, Nate," I said, drumming my fingers on the table. "I have a favor to ask. Can four of my friends tag along on your spirit trip?"

"I don't really care," Nate replied, "I hate this trip and everything to do with it anyway. What a waste of time and the society's coffers." He fell silent for a moment. "You've never been interested in football before," he said. "Does this have anything to do with your new job?"

"How do you know—"

"Mom mentioned it this morning." He paused. "So, does it?"

I sighed. "Yes, it does."

"Okay." He fell silent for a moment. "We leave tomorrow at nine o'clock. Tell your—friends—to meet us at the George Mason Library. The bus leaves from there."

"Thanks, Nate," I said, voice cracking. "I truly appreciate it."

"Sure." He hung up.

I looked up. "Okay, it's a go. Can the medic team leave from the George Mason library tomorrow at nine?"

Anna nodded briskly, gesturing to Phillip. He pulled out his phone and began to text. "It's a go," he reported after a few moments.

I frowned. "Anna ... " I said slowly. "Maybe the paranoia is talking again. But how do you know our phones aren't tapped?"

Anna laughed. "A little bit of paranoia in this business really isn't a bad thing," she replied. "This whole room is protected from eavesdropping." She raised her hand, snapping her fingers. "I'd know if someone was listening in."

"Right," I said. My heart rate returned to normal, and I put my phone down.

"Okay," Anna said, looking at the map. "So our medic team is ready to go. Now, we need to plan out supply. The medic team will have their medical supplies, of course, but we'll need to arrange to get them food."

We talked for a while, going over resupply. Phillip leaned back in his chair, eyes drooping. Garrett added the occasional comment, fingers bridged together. At last, Anna put down her pen.

"That's enough for now," she announced. "Let's get lunch."

I nodded, standing. "I brought mine," I volunteered. "I just need to go to the car and grab it."

Anna nodded, distracted. She was studying the map again. "That's fine," she murmured. She was tapping her pen on the table.

I jogged out of the room, snagging my keys on the way. I blinked. Charles was sitting in the conference room.

"Well, well," he said with a lazy smile. "If it isn't Eileen O'Donnell. Working hard, or hardly working?" His eyes trailed down my face and body.

"That's classified," I said shortly. I dangled my keys. "Right now, I'm interested in lunch."

"Is that an invitation?" Charles sat a little taller in his chair.

"Absolutely not," I replied coolly. I glanced at the table. He had a book out. "What's the book?"

He put a finger on the page he was reading and flipped it shut, holding it up to me. I looked at the title. "Sun Tzu?" I asked.

"A little professional development," he said, voice rumbling. Charles looked at me again. "Why don't we get lunch?" he suggested. "I could use a break from my book, and I bet your sandwich is wilted from all the time in the car."

"Thanks," I said, turning away, "but no thanks. I need to get back to work."

Charles laughed. "You do that, then," he said, going back to his book. "See you."

"See you," I echoed, fingering my keys. I walked

out of the room, carefully shutting the door behind me. I jogged to my car, glad I'd worn clothes I could move in. It was chilly.

I unlocked the car and froze. I could feel eyes on me. I got in the car and slammed the door, locking it, and surveyed the parking lot. There was nothing there.

Just a paranoid feeling, I told myself firmly. I grabbed my lunch from the passenger seat and resolutely jumped out. Nothing to worry about.

I jogged back to the building, stopping at the door and sighing. I knocked, eyeing the blue surrounding the door with disfavor. The door opened. Charles stood there.

"Come in, Eileen," he murmured, opening the door fully. The murmur sounded strangely intimate. I walked in, ignoring it.

"Thank you, Charles," I said, holding my keys close and my lunch in the other hand. If he attacked, I could punch him with the keys.

He seemed to know which way my thoughts were headed. His eyes crinkled and he stepped back, bowing again and gesturing toward the conference room door. "Please," he said formally. "After you."

I smiled frostily and swept ahead of him, walking steadily toward the conference room. At the door, I leaned in. "Unicorn," I whispered. The door opened.

"Don't forget to close the door behind you," Charles's voice sounded behind me. I turned around, one hand on the door. He winked at me. "You never know who's on the prowl."

I sighed. "Thank you for the advice," I said, voice still frosty. I closed the door firmly.

I walked to the War Room, wondering about Charles. I'd run into his type back in the military— a wandering eye, a handsome face, and a quick tongue made for a dangerous combination for some women. Not me, I thought firmly, whispering to the War Room. It opened smoothly, and I walked back in.

"Ah, Eileen," Anna said distractedly. It looked as though she hadn't moved. "Let's eat and talk. Or you eat and I'll talk."

"Did you not bring lunch? I can give you half my sandwich," I offered.

Resolutely, Anna shook her head. "No, thanks— it'll remind me to bring my lunch next time. Now, let's chat." She pushed the list of supplies to me. "I added a few we might need. What do you think?"

The day went by swiftly after that; after about an hour, I went to Phillip's station at the BFT, and he taught me how to work it.

"It's not so different from what you had in the army," he said, clicking with the mouse. "We just rely more on magic than the army did. Must be nice," he said wistfully, "to have satellite access."

Anna sent me home at five o'clock. "You'll have enough late nights," she said. "Get out at a reasonable time while you still can." I smiled, walking to the door. Charles was gone. I felt a small twinge and dismissed it at once. It couldn't possibly be disappointment.

CHAPTER 4

⸺◆⸺

OVER THE NEXT week, my days fell into a routine. I'd go in, mission plan with Anna, work with Phillip on the BFT, and trade snarky comments with Charles in the conference room. He always seemed to be there, though he'd moved on to a new book.

"Von Clausewitz?" I asked, as he showed me the title. "I read that. Clunky. Dull." I paused. "Irrelevant," I said wickedly.

"I'd disagree with you there," Charles said, smiling. Each time we locked eyes, his seemed to soften. "Clunky, yes. Dull, yes. Irrelevant? No." He paused. "War changes because of technological and magical innovation, but the fundamental truths don't."

I pulled out a chair and sprawled into it. "I'd argue that those technological and magical innovations do change those very fundamentals. Look at World War II. The Poles managed to hold their own because of their magical genius."

"They were eventually overrun by superior forces," Charles countered, putting his hand on the table for emphasis.

"Only because the fae—with their far superior magical sophistication—joined the Germans."

"But you just made my point. Magical superiority *is* superiority of arms. A fundamental truth of war is that he who has them, wins."

We debated for a while, until I happened to catch a glimpse of my watch. It was six thirty. I'd sat there and talked with Charles for an hour and a half. "I have to go," I said quickly, jumping to my feet.

"Of course," Charles said easily, sprawled back in his chair, his eyes still soft. "I'll see you tomorrow."

"Yes," I said, straightening my back and grabbing my purse.

"Eileen." His voice stopped me as I began to turn away. It was low, rumbling. "Do you carry pepper spray?"

"Yes," I said, frowning.

"Good. You might want to get a gun, as well."

My back stiffened. "I can't buy a gun," I snapped. "I was involuntarily committed to a mental hospital." Let him chew on that.

He laughed, soft and low. "You are such a law-abiding citizen, Eileen." I heard his chair push back as he prowled up behind me. "Leave it to me," he whispered in my ear. I jumped. He laughed again. "I'll see you tomorrow." He moved back and to the side, standing next to me. He gave a slight bow, extending his arm toward the door.

Wordless, I swept to the door, fumbling with the knob. Charles leaned over and gently pushed it open. "Thank you," I said stiffly. I marched through. I could feel the spot on my shoulder, the place Faolain had caught me with his magic, burning.

Charles's hand caught my shoulder and swung me around. He grabbed my other shoulder, holding me at an arm's length as he gazed sharply at the spot. His nostrils flared as he drew in a deep breath. His eyes went hard.

"When did that happen?" he rasped, his grip tightening.

I shifted, wondering if I should punch him. "When I fought with Faolain," I said, voice tight. "He caught me with some kind of magic."

Charles frowned. "Did you feel a wave of heat sweep through you?"

I frowned back. "I did."

Charles's grip got tighter. "Well then," he said, his voice deeper and lower, "you really need that gun." He released me suddenly. "Let me walk you to your car."

"I don't need an escort," I snapped. He smiled at me, eyes crinkling, still hard. They looked cold, I noticed, cold and dangerous.

"You do," he replied simply, putting his hand on the small of my back and urging me forward. "Let's go."

There was clearly no reasoning with him. I

marched forward, shoulders up and spine straight. Charles chuckled.

"You look like a lieutenant on a parade ground," he murmured. I glared at him. He smiled at me.

Silent, we walked out of the building. We ran into Jenny at the door, who glanced from me to Charles. Her mouth tightened.

"Charles," she said, voice dropping low, "are you still going to help me with the operations order?"

"Of course, Jenny," Charles replied, walking past her, hand still on the small of my back. Jenny scowled at me.

We walked to my car together. I took out my keys, unlocking it. Charles grabbed the door handle and opened it, gesturing to the driver's seat. "Please," he said politely.

"I can open a door myself," I snapped, swinging myself in and putting the keys in the ignition."

He chuckled. "Of course you can, Eileen. But you don't have to." He gestured. "Seat belt," he said pointedly.

I glared at him, snapping the seatbelt into the buckle. "Satisfied?" I asked.

"Not really. But it'll do for now." He closed the door.

I jerked the car into reverse, checking to make sure he was out of the way. He stood well off to the side, smiling benignly, eyes still hard. I waved, surprising myself. He blinked, then raised his hand. I peeled off into the road, gripping the wheel tightly.

What on earth was I thinking? He was trouble—lots of it, if I was any judge. Better to leave him to Jenny, I thought, giving the wheel a vicious tug. He'd get tired with me before long and move on.

Besides. I couldn't forget who I was. I was a damaged, schizophrenic former lieutenant. I couldn't see any relationship working for long, not before he got tired of my constant paranoia, occasional hallucinations, and inability to do magic.

I breathed deeply, deliberately releasing my death grip on the steering wheel. It was for the best to stay away, I told myself firmly. There was no future. There was no potential. No matter how charming his smile or compelling his eyes, they were not for me.

I sighed. I often cursed my condition, remembering who and what I was before the fight that had cost me my magic. I'd been a top caster of battle spells, slated for deployment to the Northern Wilds. I'd hoped to be one of the first female Rangers—my battle spells were certainly up to muster. I'd been working on my run and my pull-ups, focusing on getting my physical strength up to par, when disaster had struck.

I couldn't think about it. Gnawing on my lip, I guided my car down the freeway. It had happened three years ago. It might as well have happened yesterday. I gripped the steering wheel again, fighting the flood of memories.

Worthless, a voice whispered to me. Joe, I recognized, feeling dismal. *What use are you?*

"Shut up," I said, punching one hand into the steering wheel. The horn blared, and the driver next to me scowled at me and flipped me off. I gritted my teeth and reached over to my radio, turning it on. I found a classical station and focused. They were playing Chopin.

I made it home, walked through the front door. Both Nate and my mother were there, putting away groceries.

"Hey there, Eileen," Nate said, holding a pack of cookies. "Want one?" He tossed me the pack.

"I could use some chocolate," I said, taking one out. Chocolate chip. My favorite. I walked over to the cabinet, putting the cookies away. "How was your day, Nate?"

"Good. The president called me from the football match. They're having a grand old time, but your friends took off. Said something about a family emergency." Nate looked at me sharply. "Is everything all right?"

"Everything's fine," I said absently.

"Was it really a family emergency?"

I sighed. "I can't answer that."

Nate nodded. "I thought so." He bent down and pulled out a can of coffee. "We ran out of coffee."

"And creamer," my mother added from the refrigerator. She looked at me. "We do use a lot of both."

I laughed. "That we do. Nate's basically nocturnal and I'm tired all the time—and you deal with children. Between all of us, it's no surprise." I bent down to a bag and pulled out toothpaste. "I'm going to run this upstairs," I said, backing out of the kitchen. My mother nodded absently as she tried to fit a jar of jalapeño peppers in the refrigerator.

I headed up the stairs to the bathroom, putting the toothpaste next to the sink. I looked in the mirror. My brown eyes were wide and staring. I sighed and splashed my face with water. That felt better.

"Eileen," a voice behind me spoke. I jumped and whirled. A Sending cloud sparkled behind me. The voice was dark and heavy. I felt myself pale, recognizing Prince Faolain.

"Eileen O'Donnell," the voice continued. "We need to talk." It paused. "I guarantee you safety and safe passage to the Northern Sun embassy in Washington, DC. Come tonight." The sending cloud sparkled again, then disappeared, collapsing in on itself in a rush.

I stood there, terrified. Did he think me a fool? To go to the embassy? I pulled out my cell phone and punched the contact for Anna. She picked up on the third ring.

"Eileen? What's wrong?" I thought I heard Charles in the background, muttering. "No, Charles," Anna said sharply.

"Anna—I just heard from Prince Faolain. He sent a Sending." I took a deep breath. "He guaranteed me safe passage to meet with him in the embassy tonight."

"Hmm. Interesting." There was a sudden noise, and Charles was on the line.

"Eileen," he said urgently, "Don't go." There was another scuffle, and Anna was back.

"It might," she said slowly, "be a good idea to go. You say he guaranteed you safe passage?"

I nodded before realizing she couldn't see me. "Yes," I said. "He did."

She made a thoughtful noise. "He won't break his word. It's sacrosanct to the fae." She paused. "Go," she said decisively. I heard a roar in the background, then muffled words. "Calm down, Charles," Anna said. "I'm not sending her alone. Eileen, come back to base. We need to fit you with a wire. Then we'll have a car follow you." More mumbled speech. "Not you, Charles," Anna said impatiently. "You're too close to this." She paused. "Head back in, Eileen."

"Roger," I said. I hung up the phone and went back downstairs. My mother and Nate had finished putting away the groceries and were sitting in the living room, both reading. "I need to go back to the NVRA, I said slowly. "They need me for a mission."

My mother closed the book with a snap. "They need you," she said flatly, "for a mission."

I took a deep breath. "Yes."

She stared at me. "You have no magic."

I nodded. "I'm the only one who can do it."

"Well." She gestured at Nate, who shut his book as well. "We'll be following along." She crossed her arms, daring me to argue.

I threw my hands up in the air. "Fine," I said, knowing better than to argue. "But they're sending a car as well. It'll be like a convoy, going around Washington, DC." I grabbed my keys. "Let's go."

I drove back to the NVRA, radio blaring—this time pop. I felt myself tense, the familiar sense of readiness and adrenaline flowing through me. It was Go time. I wanted to confront Faolain. I wanted to look into his eyes and make him regret ever having chased Sarah and Tara, ever having fought me.

I parked. Nate and my mother drew up next to me, my mother waving at me to go inside. I walked to the door, knocking. Charles opened it, looking grim.

"Who're they?" he asked, waving at the car.

"My mother and brother," I said with a sigh.

Charles nodded, eyes bright and hard, mouth in a grim line. "It'll be a family affair, then. I'm coming too."

I frowned at him. "First of all, I heard Anna tell you no. Second, you're not family."

His expression didn't change. "I'm coming too." He led me to the conference room, whispering to it and courteously holding it open.

"I thought you didn't let anyone in after you," I joked, walking through.

"That sounds like Garrett," he said dismissively. He placed his hand on the small of my back, guiding me through the conference room. He whispered to the War Room, opening the door and holding it for me. "Go ahead," he murmured. "I'll be waiting right here."

I walked in, momentarily missing the comforting presence at my shoulder. I shook myself, deliberately willing the feeling away. Anna, Garrett, and Jenny stood in the War Room, clustered around the Sending station.

"Ah, Eileen," Garrett said, sounding distracted. One hand was on the Sending station, sending pulsing light into it. Jenny stood in front of it, speaking into it.

"You will rendezvous here in fifteen minutes," she concluded, stepping away. She nodded to Garrett, and the pulsing light stopped.

"Now," she said, stepping over to me and holding out her hand, "your wire."

It was small and black, pulsing with magic. "I've never worn a wire before," I said, fingering it.

Jenny sighed, impatient. "I'll help you put it on," she said, businesslike. Anna nodded behind her, eyes watchful. "Garrett, turn around."

Garrett obediently turned around. Jenny lifted my shirt and slapped her hand down, perhaps a little harder than necessary. I winced as the wire sparked, attaching itself to my skin.

"Test it, Garrett," Jenny barked.

Garrett's face showed no emotion, but I had the sense he was displeased. He waved his hand. "It's working, ma'am," he said after a moment.

"Good," Jenny said, looking pleased. She looked at me. "Your escort is outside." She frowned. "It's very unprofessional to have your mother and brother following you, as well." Anna sighed but said nothing.

"I'm the one going to talk with Prince Faolain," I said firmly. "I should get to say who goes."

Jenny sighed. "Fine. As long as Charles doesn't go too." She shot me a hard look.

I smiled innocently at her. "I can't control him," I said, voice sweet.

She glared. "Go, then," she said, voice poisonous.

Anna stepped forward. "Jenny, wait. She needs a briefing."

"You do it, then. You're the expert on all things Faolain." Jenny gave her a smile. Anna's face momentarily registered deep pain before she visibly pulled herself together.

"All right, Eileen," she said after a moment. "You know that Faolain is the prince of Northern Sun. That, of course, is the northern territory in the Midwest. And you know that his father is Lugh, the king." She took a deep breath and handed me a folder.

"This is all we know of Faolain, Eileen. It's not much." I flipped through the folder. The first page was a picture—clearly a surveillance photo. Faolain was dressed in a suit, entering a building. It looked like a Congressional office. I felt a chill bolt through me, and my shoulder tingled. I clapped a hand on it. Jenny's eyes lingered on the spot.

I flipped to the next page. It was a dossier. I skimmed it, frowning at parts. "So," I said slowly, "He's his father's hatchet man."

"Correct," Anna said. "He's the one who usually hunts down slaves if they make it to the city. The times we lose people or safe houses, it's usually to him."

"But the dossier says he has no personal slaves himself."

"He uses family slaves," Anna said, "but no, he has no personal slaves. Most unusual for a nobleman." She sighed. "We had hoped, when he came to DC, that he might prove an ally of sorts, based on that. We were dead wrong."

I nodded, shutting the dossier. "All right," I said, handing the folder back. "Let's move."

I walked back out to my car. My spirits sank when I didn't see Charles, but I shoved the disappointment away. I had a mission to complete. I gave my mother the thumbs-up. She nodded, and Nate gunned the engine.

I slid in, and then spotted a note on my dash-board. I frowned. The car had been locked. I carefully unfolded it.

Check your trunk - C

Getting out, I walked around to my trunk and opened it. There was a small box in it, gift wrapped in blue paper with a blue bow taped on top. I took it back to the front seat and carefully opened it. My breath caught. It was a pistol. Quickly, I checked the magazine and the safety. The safety was on, but the pistol was loaded. I held it, checking the weight, the balance, and the grip. It was perfect.

I gently placed it in the passenger side seat, ejecting the magazine and tossing it into the back seat. There. Now I was legal. I pulled out of the spot, waving at my mother and Nate. My mother's eyebrows were raised.

The drive to the embassy seemed to take forever. I checked the time when I pulled up to the embassy—seven forty-five. It'd barely been a thirty-minute drive but seemed to have taken hours. I paused. Should I take the pistol? I doubted they'd let me bring it in. Frowning, I left it where it was, putting an old T-shirt from my gym bag on top of it.

The embassy was a large building, a stately Georgian home with a valet. I got out of the car, leaving it running, and reluctantly handed my keys to the human valet. I didn't like losing control of my car but took comfort in knowing that I was being tailed by at least two cars. "I'm expected," I told him. He nodded silently and got in my car. As he did, I could've sworn he cast me a sympathetic look from his downturned eyes.

I walked to the front door, breathing slightly hard, and knocked. The door opened. A stately fae stood there, his long black hair swept back in a French braid, his robes black and scarlet. The Northern Sun coat of arms was embroidered over his heart. "Eileen O'Donnell," I said, staring directly into his eyes. "I'm expected."

He nodded, saying nothing, and stood to the side, opening the door wider. I squared my shoulders and walked in. "Where is Prince Faolain?" I asked.

"Here," a deep, growling voice sounded. I looked up. There was a wide set of stairs in the entry hall, which Faolain was descending. He'd traded the armor for a magnificent robe, also black and scarlet, with a wide sash crossing his right shoulder. It was embroidered in gold with the coat of arms. He wore his hair back, also in a French braid, and had a circlet on his head.

"Eileen O'Donnell." He stopped in front of me and looked directly at me. I stared back, feeling pressure behind my eyes. Faolain frowned intently, eyes moving slowly over my face. "I see that you dressed up," he said dryly.

I looked down. I was wearing what I'd gone to work in—black pants, a grey sweater with a hood, and black boots. My hair was in a bun at the back of my head. "You're lucky I didn't show up in sweat-pants," I shot back.

Faolain frowned harder. I felt the pressure behind my eyes build, and I blinked. The pressure eased, and Faolain's lips pursed. "This way," he said sourly, gesturing to the right.

I followed him to a small room off the hall. It was elegantly appointed, scarlet curtains pulled back with golden ties, uncomfortable wooden chairs sitting next to the windows. Prince Faolain gestured me into one. "Please, sit," he said. I sat, lacing my hands in front of me and crossing my legs. Faolain frowned again and then followed suit, copying my body posture. "I need to know how you did what you did back in McConnell Consultants."

I blinked. "Did what? Punch you in the face?"

"No," he snapped. I noticed that his nose looked completely normal, an elegant Roman blade that Michelangelo would've begged to carve. "The bond. How did you initiate it?"

"What bond?" I blinked again. He sighed, impatient.

"You know what you did, Eileen O'Donnell. You feel the bond." Faolain leaned forward. "Undo it. This is no good for either of us."

"I ... didn't initiate a bond." The spot on my shoulder twinged again. I frowned as I felt a burn spread through my body. I looked at Faolain sharply.

"What are you doing?"

"I'm doing nothing, Eileen O'Donnell." He spat my name out, as though it tasted bad. "You did it."

"I have no magic, if you didn't notice," I said coldly, rising to my feet.

"I know the story." Faolain remained seated. "You were in the army. One of your soldiers was in a fight with someone. You stepped in and took a sharp blow to the head." He paused. "You didn't go in for medical treatment for almost a week."

I sat back down. "How did you get ahold of my medical records?" I asked angrily.

"I have my ways." Faolain could have been carved from stone. "Now. You have no magic. How did you initiate the bond?"

"Perhaps *I* didn't," I snapped. "Perhaps *you* did. Perhaps you're not as in control as you think you are. And you haven't explained what a bond is."

"Are you dense?" Faolain's voice was cold and cutting. "What use would I have for you? And a bond ... " he paused, as though searching for the right words, "... it draws us together. Eventually, we'll be able to speak mind-to-mind."

I leaned forward. "You've got to be kidding me."

Faolain smiled. "No. I'm not. And I've been practicing magic for well over two hundred years—I assure you, I did not lose control." He paused again, then leaned forward. Out of nowhere, he grabbed my arm—just like he had in our fight. I screamed and leaned back. It was too late. Energy flooded through me, burning, cutting. I felt the wire on my skin spark.

"So," Faolain said softly, releasing my hand. "It's all true. You have no magic." He put his hand to his head, running it down his braid in thought.

"As I told you," I said angrily. "You gave me your word that I'd have safe passage, and safety while I was here."

"So I did," Faolain said lazily. "Are you accusing me of breaking it? That's a serious accusation, you know. You'd have to take me to a Court of Honor." He smiled, his teeth flashing. "We'd see how they'd rule—a human against a fae prince?" He paused. "But, as it happens," he murmured, "I didn't break my word. That was to answer a question, nothing more—and if you'd specified that, my dear, I would've kept my word. Don't blame me that neither your nor your advisors can think." His gaze swept down my body. "And I'm afraid your little wire is out. Clever, but not clever enough ... very few technological things can stand up to the full might of a fae prince."

I swallowed. "When will we begin hearing mind-to-mind?" I asked.

"It depends." He laced his fingers together again. "A year? Two? Ten? There's no way to know. It depends on how sympathetic are magics are."

"I have none."

"Not quite," he said, lifting a finger in admonishment. "You have it. You just can't use it. Your prefrontal cortex is damaged." Faolain paused. "If you were fae, your body would've adapted by now. Built new neural passageways to allow the impulses to flow. Fortunately for me," his teeth flashed in a smile, "you're not fae." He stood abruptly.

"This little audience is finished," he murmured. "Eileen O'Donnell." He swept his hand to the door.

"Prince Faolain," I said, voice tight. I turned to the door and marched out. *A lieutenant on a parade ground*, Charles's voice echoed in my head.

The fae who had opened the door was waiting for me. "Eileen O'Donnell," he said coldly. "You were invited. Your guest was not."

I blinked. "Guest?"

The fae swung the door open. Charles stood there, at parade rest, eyes fixed unblinkingly on the door. He saw me, and his eyes lightened, though they never lost their hard edge.

"Let's go," he growled, reaching for my arm. I stumbled and he caught me, waiting until I got my feet back under me. I swallowed.

"Let's go," I agreed. We walked together down the stairs, where the valet waited with my car. I swung in and blinked. Charles was seated in the passenger seat.

"What about your car?" I asked in astonishment.

"Don't worry about it," he growled. "What possessed you to give your car to the valet?"

I swallowed. "There was nowhere to park, and I knew I was being tailed—"

"You should've parked in the damn driveway," he snapped. His eyes flashed. "You gave up your means of escape."

I nodded weakly. He was right.

"Just drive," he said, sounding disgusted. I noticed that he had my pistol in his lap. "And," he added, voice dangerous, "I reloaded your pistol."

I nodded again and did as he said—drove.

CHAPTER 5

I DIDN'T STOP DRIVING until I reached the NVRA. Charles sat silently next to me, one hand on my pistol, the other lying casually next to the window. He constantly checked the driver's mirror and the left and right mirrors.

"You're as paranoid as I am," I said flippantly, trying to lighten the atmosphere.

"Worse," he growled, eyes flicking from window to window. I pulled into the parking lot at the NVRA and he jumped out. "Stay there," he ordered. My mother's car pulled in next to mine, followed by the tail I'd been assigned. Charles grunted with satisfaction, coming around to the driver's door and opening it. I eyed him but allowed him to hand me out.

"Time for debrief," he murmured. He stuck the pistol in my hand "Keep that. And get a holster."

"It's a kind gift," I said slowly, "but I don't think Faolain wants to kill me."

"And his enemies?" Charles snapped. He patted the pistol. "Keep it. Don't lose it. And use it if you need it." His hand at the small of my back, he guided me through the door. "Have dinner with me," he said, not looking at me.

I swallowed. "I can't," I said, voice flat.

"Why not?" His voice was full of mocking laughter. "Jealous boyfriend?"

"No," I said, voice heavy. "You forget I'm a schizophrenic, magic-less former lieutenant with nothing to offer. I'd just hurt you."

He growled. "That's the biggest load of bullshit I've ever heard." He leaned into the conference door, whispering his password and ushering me through. "You're smart. You have intelligent but misguided views on the science of war. You're capable, except when you forget your weapon when meeting a potential enemy. Have dinner with me."

I swallowed. "No promises," I warned him.

"No promises," he agreed. His hand tightened on the small of my back. "Let's get this debrief over with. How does tomorrow night, seven o'clock work? I'll pick you up."

"Sounds good," I said, feeling hopeless. This would end badly, I was sure of it.

He whispered to the door of the War Room. It opened, and I went through. Jenny, Phillip, Anna, and Garrett were all standing around the BFT, staring at it.

"See, the forces aren't moving," Phillip said, pointing at the BFT. "The safe house reports all clear. I think we're okay." He looked up and saw me with

Charles. "Ah, Eileen," he said, sounding relieved. "That was tense." He gestured at Jenny. "Let's get the wire off." He, Garrett, and Charles politely turned away as I lifted my shirt, and Jenny took off the wire. *That was more of a rip*, I thought, staring at her as she tucked the ruined wire in an envelope. I wondered what her problem was but sighed as her eyes flicked to Charles. Of course it would be that.

"All right," Anna said, clapping her hands. "Let's start, shall we?" She motioned to the conference table. We all sat down around it—Charles next to me, Anna at the head as she played with her pen. "We all heard what was happening, Eileen," she continued, "Up to the time Faolain destroyed your wire." She paused. "What happened next?"

"He said ... " I took a deep breath "... that eventually we'd be able to speak mind-to-mind." Beside me, Charles shifted restlessly. His hands were clasped tightly, and he was staring at the center of the table.

"I see," Anna murmured. Her face had gone white. "Did he say when that would happen?"

"No," I replied, clenching my own fists. "He said it depended on the compatibility of our magic."

"This is a security violation," Jenny interrupted, pointing her finger at me. "She needs to go." She looked a little triumphant. I swallowed.

"I understand if I have to go," I said, trying to keep my voice from cracking. I began to rise. Charles's hand clasped my wrist and pulled me back down.

"No," he said, in a tone that brooked no arguments. "You don't." He looked at Anna. "She hasn't heard him yet," he pointed out, "and it could be a valuable asset."

Anna frowned, drumming her pen on the table again. "You're correct," she said slowly, "assuming she doesn't give any information to him. By accident, of course," she added, turning to me.

"Yes," I said, lips numb.

"This could be valuable to the war," Garrett said. "A way into the enemy's mind? Properly controlled, it could be a great help to us."

"But how will I keep him from knowing about me?" I interjected.

"We have methods," Anna said, a gleam in her eye. "Charles," she glanced at him, "can you teach them to her?"

"With pleasure," he murmured. He still hadn't released my wrist. "We'll start tonight."

I felt the stirrings of hope. "There are methods?" I asked, turning to Charles. He was looking at me, eyes soft once more.

"There are," he acknowledged. "They take willpower, focus, and mental strength. You've already beaten a Truth spell"—he gestured at Jenny, who frowned angrily—"so I have no doubt you can also beat Faolain." Anna's face registered pain, once more, at the mention of Faolain's name.

"With that, then," she said, regaining control

of herself, "we're dismissed. Be back tomorrow at nine." She stood. "Unless, Eileen, you and Charles are up all night working on your barrier. Just text me." She exited the War Room, followed by Garrett. Jenny lingered.

"This is a mistake, Charles," she said, looking at me. "She could endanger everything we've worked for."

"Could," Charles agreed, "but won't." His hand pressed my wrist harder. "That's why I'm going to teach her the tricks."

Jenny sighed and followed Garrett and Anna out. There was silence for a moment in the War Room as I stared at Charles, and Charles stared back. His mouth curved into a smile.

"All right, then, Eileen," he murmured. "Shall we begin?"

I nodded.

"Defend yourself, then," he snapped, his eyes flashing as I suddenly felt pressure behind my eyes. I yelped and automatically gestured, my old training in battle magic resurfacing.

"Not that way, Eileen," Charles said, looking sad for a moment. "Push me out of your mind." A memory flashed by, of me getting dressed that morning. "Or I'll get to see more," he said with a wicked smile.

I focused, remembering the feeling I'd had earlier with Faolain. "Did Faolain read my mind?" I asked in horror. "The feeling was exactly like this."

"He probably tried," Charles acknowledged, "but one benefit of the wire—it has magic that interrupts mind-reading attempts. It's probably how he knew you were wearing one, when his attempts didn't work." His eyes hardened. "You can't rely on it. Now. Defend yourself!" I was back in my room, dressing.

"Stop," I gasped, trying to cast another spell.

"Your magic is gone, Eileen, and Faolain won't stop if you ask him to." The pressure behind my eyes faded, and Charles sighed. "You have to push me out, Eileen," he explained. "I won't just leave." His eyes flickered, and for a moment, it seemed there was a double meaning there. I filed it away for closer examination later.

He's going to hurt you, Joe's voice remarked.

He will, Sheldon agreed.

"No, I won't," Charles murmured. His eyes were steady on mine. I felt the pressure against my eyes again.

"Tell them to shut the hell up" Charles said. "They don't know anything." I hesitated. "Tell them!"

"Shut ... shut up, Joe and Sheldon," I muttered.

"Not very convincing," Charles said with a sigh, "But better than nothing." His eyes flickered, and I realized he was hurt.

"Charles," I said, reaching over and grasping his hand, "I can't control the voices. And most of the time, they lie."

He stared at my hand, then exhaled, moving his other hand to cover mine. "Is it time to take your medicine?" he asked, voice gravelly.

I pulled out my cell phone and glanced at the clock. "Nine thirty. Yes it is." I grabbed the Clozaril and dry swallowed it, trying not to retch.

"You know, Eileen," Charles remarked mildly, "you could've asked for water." He pulled out a bottle and set it in front of me. I blinked and swallowed it down.

"Thank you," I murmured.

"No problem." We were both silent for a moment. "Now," he ordered, "push me out." I felt the pressure behind my eyes again.

I frowned. Push him out ... I focused on the pressure, imagining it leaking out through my eyes, like teardrops.

"Almost," Charles said, voice gravelly. "Push harder." The pressure intensified.

I pictured, this time, a wall, like a dam, pushing back against the pressure. I pushed on the wall, making it move forward. It reminded me of the trash compactor scene in *Star Wars*. Slowly, the pressure began to wane.

"Good," Charles murmured. The pressure completely vanished. "Now, you need to do it faster." He stood abruptly and extended a hand to me. "Which we will work on tomorrow. You've had a long day." Slowly, I took his hand. My head throbbed.

"I'll drive you home, Eileen." Charles held his hand out for my keys. I stared at him.

"Why on earth would you do that?" My head pounded in time with my words.

He raised his eyebrows. "You're exhausted—I can tell. It's not safe for you to drive."

"I can drive myself," I muttered, embarrassed. He sighed.

"Eileen, you can barely keep your eyes open." He swallowed. "Please," he said with some difficulty. "Let me drive you home."

I sighed. "Fine," I muttered, dumping my keys in his hand. "If you insist."

"Thank you," Charles said gravely. "I truly appreciate it." He put his hand at my back again, guiding me out the door. I stumbled, barely able to walk. He caught me and slung his arm around my shoulders. "Do I need to carry you?" he asked.

I laughed, then realized he was entirely serious. "No," I said. "No, I'm capable of walking."

"If you're sure," he murmured. He guided me through the conference room, out into the parking lot. Nate and my mother were still parked there, but the tail car had taken off.

"You forgot this." He handed me my pistol. "You really need a holster."

"Yes, sir," I said demurely.

"You're mocking me," Charles muttered.

"Damn straight I am."

He laughed. "Good to know you still have your spirit." He guided me to the car and opened the passenger door, holding my arm as I leveraged myself into it. He closed the door behind me and headed around to the driver's side of the car. He lowered himself in, locking the doors. "Now tell me," Charles said casually, "what you think of this latest proposal to end the sanctuary law."

I snorted. "Corey Hamilton is a Class A douche." I leaned back in my seat. "That proposal is a disaster."

We talked about the sanctuary law as we pulled out of the parking lot, Nate and my mother tailing us. Charles was telling me a story about Corey Hamilton when he stiffened.

"Hello, there," he murmured. "We're being followed."

I frowned. "What? By who?" I checked the window. A dark green car with tinted windows was following my mother's car.

"Who do you think?" Charles shrugged. "Faolain must really not want you to feel safe." He sighed. "We might as well drive straight back to your place. He knows where you live. This is him, testing the boundaries, seeing how we'll respond—he knows that a full-scale attack on you would be a disaster."

"But," I said slowly, "Faolain can't kill me. The other fae said it, at McConnell Consultants—if Faolain kills me, he dies too."

Charles looked at me sharply. "That's true," he agreed, voice neutral. "It also doesn't make much sense that he'd guarantee your safety, let you walk into the embassy, and let you walk out again if he wanted to hold you captive." His nostrils flared. "Unlike Anna and Garrett, I don't hold a high opinion of that particular fae's sense of honor." He frowned. "What do you think?"

I sighed. "Maybe it's not Faolain. Didn't you say earlier that he had enemies?"

"I did," Charles agreed. "Some of them almost as powerful as Faolain." He stared at the mirror again, drumming his fingers on the steering wheel. "Let's drive back to your house," he murmured. "Let's see what they do."

We drove back to my house, the tinted green car still following. But as we pulled into the housing development, the green car sped away. Charles watched it go with a frown.

"That's strange," he said. His eyes cut to me. "I'm staying with you tonight."

"Oh, you are?" I felt my ire rise. "If you think we're sleeping together—"

"No, no," he interrupted hastily, "I wouldn't dare presume." He looked over at me, eyes dancing. "I might find myself missing a pair of balls." I laughed in spite of myself.

"No," Charles continued seriously. "There may be a new, unknown player in the game. I want you to be safe." His breath caught. "Will you—let me—stay tonight?"

I frowned. "We only have the couch—"

"No problem," he said, with a dismissive wave of his hand. "That'll be fine."

I sighed. "Fine," I said grudgingly. I sighed again. I had to give credit where credit was due. "I—appreciate—all your help."

He went dead silent, staring out the windshield. One hand covered mine. "Thank you," he said simply. "Thank you for letting me."

He parked the car and got out, looking around. Nate and my mother pulled in behind us. "So this is where you live?" Charles asked with curiosity. "Who lives here?"

"My brother. My mother. My father. I have another brother, but he works on an oil platform in the Gulf Sea."

Charles frowned. "In the Kingdom of Texas?"

"Yes, on one of the contracted platforms."

"I see." He went silent as my mother and Nate got out of the car.

"Mrs. O'Donnell," Charles said, extending his hand. "I'm Charles Talbot."

My mother shook his hand. "Nice to meet you," she said. Nate came up next to her.

"My younger brother, Nate," I said, waving at him. Charles shook his hand.

"I'm staying the night—with your permission, of

course, Mrs. O'Donnell—for protection," Charles said, lowering his hand. "May I ask, ma'am, where your husband is?"

"My husband is on a trip to Finland," my mother said. "But why do you ask?"

"Well—it would provide extra protection—"

My mother's eyes narrowed. "Charles," she said politely, "I'm former law enforcement. I know how to shoot a gun, and I was the one who helped Eileen review her battle magic. I assure you I'm more than capable of protecting the house."

"Yes ma'am," Charles said, sounding awkward, "but I hope you have no objection to me staying as well?"

My mother narrowed her eyes, studying him. "None," she said after a moment, "provided you sleep on the couch."

"Of course, ma'am," Charles rushed to reassure her, "not a problem at all."

My mother nodded decisively. "That's fine, then," she said, sweeping into the house. Nate followed, looking thoughtful.

Charles and I were left standing outside in the driveway, looking at each other. "Eileen," he said after a moment, "can I ask why you live with your family?"

"Why shouldn't I?" I asked, feeling defensive.

"No reason," he said calmly. "I just wondered if it had something to do with your disabilities."

I sighed. "You're right," I said after a moment. "I love my family, but I live here partly because of my disabilities." I paused. "I had a breakdown," I said, voice tight. "Got fired from my job, since I had it at work. I started hallucinating, thinking people were following me. I heard voices, saw images. It was terrible."

Charles nodded thoughtfully and took my hand. It was strangely comforting. "Do they think it's from your injury?"

"Nobody knows," I said, shaking my head. "I never had any problems before my injury, but schizophrenia is supposed to be genetic."

He sighed. "I heard about how your injury happened." He paused. "Eileen—do you think it's possible you were cursed with schizophrenia?"

I frowned. "Cursed? Who would curse me?"

"Eileen, you broke up a fight between one of your soldiers and someone else." Charles looked at me carefully. "Was there more to it than that?"

I sighed. "Let's go inside," I said, waving at the door. Charles and I walked there together, his eyes alert. He was still holding my hand. I opened the door with my key and led him to the sofa. My mother was in the kitchen, making tea. Nate was probably in his room.

"I was the officer in charge of a training mission," I began, throat tight, "when a soldier approached me. She told me she was being sexually harassed by an officer, one of my friends, back at post." I paused. "I immediately filed a report, but there wasn't enough to go on. She refused to participate in the investigation—she told me she was scared. But when we got back to post, she changed. She acted terrified, like someone was out to get her." I stopped again and cleared my throat. "One night," I said slowly, "I got a call from this soldier. She asked me to come to her house. She said she was scared. So I went." I sighed. "I got there, and the officer—Lieutenant Daniels—was there. He was outside her house, shouting at her. It was like he'd completely lost it. The soldier saw me and came out. She thought I'd protect her. But he saw her and threw himself at her—went straight for her throat. I tried to pull him off and he hit me, really hard, on the head. I went unconscious." I cleared my throat again. "I woke up to find Daniels gone, my soldier dead, and my head aching."

Charles nodded. "I read the police report," he said quietly. "They found him two counties over."

I nodded. "They did. I testified at his trial. He's in prison now, serving life."

Charles leaned forward. "Thank you," he said, voice rough, "for talking to me."

I nodded quietly. We sat there together for a moment, until I sighed.

"That wasn't the only time I intervened," I said quietly. "Just the most physical. It was part of the reason I wanted to become an advocate when I got out—I'd seen so much anger and violence in the army."

Charles nodded silently. We sat there quietly for a few more moments before he pulled back and sighed. "You should go to bed," he said gently. "We did hard work today."

I nodded and laughed. "We certainly did." I ran my hand over my forehead. "Let me get you a pillow and a blanket."

I grabbed them both from an upstairs closet and turned around to find him right behind me. He gently grabbed my shoulders and pulled me toward him, giving me a long, gentle kiss. I sighed, feeling myself sag. The kiss turned deeper, more passionate. His tongue nudged at my lips; I opened them, feeling his tongue slide into my mouth. I wasn't about to be a passive recipient. I matched his tongue with mine, daring him to give me more. He moaned softly, holding me tighter, as our tongues danced.

At last, he drew away. "Good night," he rumbled, eyes dark, holding mine in a gaze almost as intimate as our kiss.

"Good night," I murmured, leaning forward and gently kissing him on the cheek. He started. I smiled, opening the door to my room. "This, you don't get to see," I said. "Sleep well." I left him standing in the hall, gaze drilling into my back, as I closed the door to my room.

I shivered, as though his gaze was still on me. I quickly undressed and flipped off the lights, stumbling my way to my bed until I could pull the covers over my head. I thought of him downstairs, lying on the couch, and shivered again. For a moment I'd forgotten about Faolain, our meeting today, and the strange car following me.

It's not going anywhere, I reminded myself. *I have a lot to overcome*. I sighed. At least I could dream.

As I drifted off to sleep, my last thoughts were memories of that kiss we'd shared—the passion, the intensity. I smiled, touching my lips, and let sleep claim me.

CHAPTER 6

⸻ ◆ ⸻

I HAD STRANGE DREAMS all night—dreams where I was chased, where I fell out of a plane, where a strange man grabbed me and held me. But in each dream there was Charles—always there, always a comforting presence. I woke smiling slightly. In the last dream Charles and I had been kissing, slowly, passionately.

He's not for you, Sheldon whispered in my mind. *You'll never have him.*

"I know," I said out loud, sighing softly. Dreams were fine, but I could not deny reality. I got up and padded to my mirror. My long brown hair was in disarray, my brown eyes wide and still faintly star-struck. My skin, usually pale, was flushed. I took a long look at myself, pulling on my shirt. It was an old university T-shirt, from when I'd been a student at the University of Fair Isle. Considered one of the best universities in the thirteen states, it also had a stellar Reserve Officer Training Corps program. It was were I'd earned my commission. It seemed so long ago, now. A completely different lifetime.

I sighed, smoothing down my sweatpants. Not bothering to fix my hair, I walked out of my room and into the hallway. I glanced down at the sofa. Charles was awake, sitting there with a steaming cup of coffee, flipping through his phone.

"Any news?" I asked, coming down the stairs. He looked up at me and smiled—tenderly, I realized with a jolt.

"Good morning to you too." Getting up from the sofa, he walked up to me and traced my face. He bent down for a kiss—I stopped him with a hand to his chest.

"Not while I have morning breath," I said with a slight laugh. He nodded, eyes grave.

"As you wish," Charles said. He waved his hand toward the kitchen. "I made coffee."

I felt myself smile at him, a gentle, tender smile. "You know the way to my heart," I said with a slight laugh. He gazed back, mouth slightly open. I stepped back and laughed uncomfortably. "Thank you."

Charles shook himself visibly and gave me a soft smile back. "Of course, Eileen," he murmured. My name sounded like a caress, coming from his mouth.

It was my turn to shake myself. I turned and went into the kitchen, filling up my favorite mug—a mug from a vacation to Chincoteague, home of the wild horses—with the coffee steaming in the pot. I loaded it down with creamer and took an appreciative sip. Tingles shot down to my toes.

"That's quite a reaction," Charles observed from the door. I smiled into the cup.

"Back in the army, I drank six cups a day," I said with a laugh. "One of my soldiers gave me a bag of coffee for a birthday present."

"Oh?" Charles asked, raising his eyebrows.

"Yes," I said, still smiling. "She was originally from Guatemala, and she went on a trip to visit her family there. When she came back, she brought me this giant"—I laughed, holding my hands wide for emphasis—"bag of coffee. She said it'd be enough to keep me busy for at least a week."

Charles laughed, eyes thoughtful. "Usually soldiers only give gifts to leaders they like and trust," he observed.

I sighed. "When I left my company, my soldiers gave me a hand-carved award thanking me for my compassion and dedication." I lifted my shoulders in a shrug. "I don't know about leadership, but I gave a damn." I lifted my coffee to my lips and took another sip. Charles watched me for a moment.

"I was an officer, as well," he said. "In the seventy-fifth Ranger Regiment." He paused. "I deployed five times—twice to the Northern Wild, once to Afghanistan, and twice to Iraq." He smiled. "The first time I was platoon leader. Then I was promoted to XO. Then I was a commander."

I raised my eyebrows. "You were a commander in the seventy-fifth Ranger Regiment?"

He nodded. "I was." He paused again. "I did a lot of shit, Eileen." He gave me a challenging look. "Also, I outrank you."

I laughed at him. "Just try to pull that card—see how far it gets you." I sipped my coffee again.

"We'll see." Charles drummed his fingers on the side of his coffee cup. "So you were an ordnance officer. What did you do?"

I smiled. "I was a platoon leader—which I loved. Then a maintenance control officer—which I hated. Then I had my accident." I sighed. "I was pretty much useless after that."

"I highly doubt that." Charles took another sip of coffee. "Why didn't you get promoted past lieutenant?"

I shrugged. "I was in a medical board—they were looking over my files to see if I'd even stay in the army. My accident." I took another sip of coffee, to fortify myself. "It took a year to finally leave the army. And only a month before my regular discharge date."

Charles nodded, eying me. "Did you go through explosive ordnance disposal school?" he asked mildly.

I froze. "I did," I said, staring at him. "I also failed out."

"That school has a high attrition rate," he said. "I think around 80 percent of its students fail."

I shrugged. "I just wasn't suited for disposing of explosives."

"No," he said quietly. "You're good with people. Analysis. You'd have made a good operations officer." Charles squinted at me. "You're in a good spot now, Eileen," he said with conviction. "The NVRA will make full use of your talents." He gave me a wolfish smile, one that made me shiver.

"I'm enjoying it so far," I said quickly, walking back to the coffee pot. I heard a sound behind me and twisted. Charles had prowled up behind me.

"Why wouldn't you?" he asked softly. "It's—challenging. And you're ambitious. Any fool can see that." His eyes traced my face, and he lifted his hand to my neck, pulling me close.

"Morning breath," I reminded him, my pulse quickening.

Charles smiled wolfishly again. "I'll risk it," he murmured, lowering his face slowly to mine.

I strained up to meet him. "This can only end in disaster," I murmured against his mouth.

"Hasn't anyone told you?" he laughed. "I'm an expert at managing disasters." Charles moved his hands so his thumb was cradling my face, and he kissed me.

Just like the previous night, the kiss was passionate. This time, though, it felt different—full of fury. I gasped, breaking away. Charles smirked and let me, still cradling my face. "Charles," I said, breath coming in gasps. "You've got to remember. I'm disabled. Everyone says you're a hound dog. There's no way this can work."

"Why don't you let me show you just how much of a hound dog I can be?" He nipped my ear. I gasped, arching back. He caught my shoulders, pulling me into a tight embrace.

"You're fierce," he said softly. "You're kind. You're smart. Name one thing I could find wrong with you."

I blinked. "Is—that a trick question?"

"You *would* turn it into one," Charles muttered, and kissed me again.

We were still kissing when I heard a cough. Gasping, I turned away and saw my mother standing in the entrance to the kitchen.

"Bit early for that," she said mildly. She pointed at the clock. I peered at it. It was five forty-five.

"I apologize, Mrs. O'Donnell," Charles said formally, loosening his hands but not releasing them.

My mother nodded and poured herself a cup of coffee. "Good coffee," she commented. She looked sternly at Charles. "And how did your first date go?"

Charles blinked. "We ... haven't had it yet."

"I see." My mother sounded disapproving. She glanced at me. "Perhaps you two should go out to dinner."

"Yes ma'am." Charles said, sounding slightly harassed. "We're going out tonight for dinner." The look he shot me made my toes curl.

"I see." My mother studied him in silence for a moment. "I'd like to speak to my daughter alone, if you don't mind."

Clara Martin

"Of course, ma'am." With one last, lingering look, he left the room, taking his coffee cup with him. After he left, my mother set hers down with a clunk.

"Eileen, I like him. But—" she hesitated. "He is acting very possessive and protective, and how long have you two known each other?"

"About two weeks," I said with a sigh. Her fears echoed mine.

"Just be careful," my mother said softly.

"I will be," I assured her. "I'll be very careful."

"Good." She took a sip of her coffee. "Storybook character parade today at school," she remarked.

We chatted about the storybook parade and her students for the next ten minutes, until she looked up at the clock. "Time to get ready for school," she remarked. As she left the kitchen, she turned and looked at me. "Remember what I said, Eileen." I nodded seriously.

Charles was waiting outside the kitchen, leaning casually against the wall, still sipping his coffee. "All right?" he asked, raising an eyebrow.

I nodded casually. "Just fine," I said, smiling hesitantly. He reached for me, but I stepped back. "I'd better get dressed," I said, heading upstairs. Charles's hand fell back to his side, and he watched me with hooded eyes as I made my way up the stairs.

Once in my room, I stripped off my sweatpants and T-shirt, and shivered. Everything was so confusing. I didn't know what to do.

Moving quickly, I picked out a pair of khakis and a button-up blue flannel shirt. I buttoned it, enjoying its softness, and then went into the bathroom. My hand hovered over my mascara for a moment before I snorted in disgust. I never wore makeup. This was ridiculous. Defiantly, I turned to the mirror and began to forcefully brush out my hair. The voices muttered in my head, too low to be heard.

My hair brushed, I braided it quickly and looped it into a bun. It was a style I'd worn in the army, and I took comfort from its familiarity. The severity emphasized my cheekbones. I made a face at myself in the mirror before turning resolutely and leaving the bathroom, grabbing my brown knee-high boots as I went. I rarely wore them, and they still smelled of new leather.

Look at her, Joe snickered in my head. *All dressed up for her date.*

"Go away," I growled, shaking my head fiercely to dislodge the voice. I felt a strand of hair uncurl from my bun and land on my face.

We'll always be with you, Sheldon chimed in. *You can never leave us behind, not really.*

"Go away," I growled, grabbing my purse. I paused outside the door to put on my boots and looked up. Charles was standing there, frowning slightly.

"Ready to go?" he asked, extending his hand.

I looked at it for a moment and then gingerly put my hand in his. "Let's go," I said, smiling.

"We can stop for more coffee on the way."

My smile grew bigger. "Franconi's?" I asked, naming the coffee shop on the corner. It was expensive, and I rarely went.

Charles's smile was affectionate. "You'll splurge on coffee, huh?"

I blinked at him. "Of course," I said. "I take my coffee seriously."

"Well, I'm buying."

"You are not," I objected. "I wouldn't have named the most expensive coffee house in town if I thought you were buying."

He looked at me, eyes heated, and gently brought my hand to his lips, kissing it. "I," he said, voice just as heated as his eyes, "am buying." He smiled, a smile full of teeth at odds with his gentle kiss.

I sighed. "I guess I'm not convincing you otherwise, am I?" I asked.

"No, you are not." He handed me the keys. "I will, however, concede to allowing you to drive."

"Allowing me?!" I stared at him. "It's my car!"

He laughed. "Fine, Eileen, but it's under protest."

We went downstairs. My mother had gone. Nate wasn't up yet. I hitched my purse over my shoulder and gestured. "Let's go, then."

His hand clasped mine tighter. "One more thing. You need that holster. Today."

"I'm not licensed to carry concealed."

He sighed. "Regrettably. What were you thinking, Lieutenant?" His voice stressed the rank. "But you don't have to carry concealed. It's legal to just carry."

I sighed. "If I end up in jail," I said halfheartedly, "you're posting bail."

Charles laughed. "Of course," he said, caressing my palm with his thumb. "Now. Franconi's."

We got in the car. It started smoothly. Charles stared out the window, tapping his fingers on the dashboard.

"What did your mother say?" he asked abruptly.

I glanced at him. "She warned me about your possessiveness, protectiveness, and moving too fast."

He snorted. "She's not wrong." His finger tapped another tattoo on the dashboard. It sounded like the army's "Reveille." "You were stationed at Fort Irwin, were you not? California."

I blinked. "I was," I said slowly.

He nodded. "It was in your record," he said by way of explanation. "You were stationed there with Rangers."

"I was," I agreed. My fingers tightened on the steering wheel. This was dangerous territory.

"Your name," he said slowly, "pops up as a complainant on a sexual harassment complaint. Along with two other lieutenants, both female. You accused a master sergeant. Master Sergeant Milagros."

"We did," I said, resigned. "Nothing came of it but no-contact orders."

"I don't know about that," Charles said. He tapped out "Reveille" again. "His career ended a year later."

I glanced at him. "Did it?"

"Yes, it did." He glanced at me. "I knew him, before he was reassigned." He paused. "Was it really just sexual harassment?" he asked delicately.

"Why do you ask?" I gripped the steering wheel.

"You're a little afraid of me," Charles said, leaning back in his seat. "And you're passionate about sexual harassment and abuse. Your history proves that."

"I don't need to be a victim to intervene, Charles. It's just the right thing to do."

He nodded. "What happened?" he asked bluntly.

I sighed. "I can't talk about it without telling the stories of the other two lieutenants, and I don't want to do that."

"Master Sergeant Milagros was a piece of shit. It wasn't the first investigation into him, and it probably wouldn't have been the last, if you three hadn't stood up." Charles paused. "Hell of a way to begin your army career."

"It was," I agreed. "But we got through it." I frowned. "It was just harassment," I said quietly. "There was nothing worse than that."

Charles looked at me, then leaned back. "If you say so."

I gripped the steering wheel. "You already know all my secrets," I said harshly. "Why don't you tell me one of yours."

He smiled, eyes half-closed. "I wondered when you'd ask." He paused for a moment. "My first deployment was in the Northern Wild. I ran into one of the wild fae—just me and my battle buddy, Santos." He smirked. "It didn't end the way I thought it would for the big, bad Ranger."

"What do you mean?" I asked, curious.

"I wet my pants," he said complacently. "The wild fae threw me against a tree—almost through it, truth be told. I was knocked out." He glanced at me. "I came to and found the wild fae crouched over Santos, eating his leg. Santos was still alive. I wet my pants."

I blinked. "Did you two—escape?"

"Well I did, obviously." Charles's eyes were still half-closed. "Santos—well. I fought the wild fae. It was hand-to-hand combat, and I was so damn scared. But Santos had died of blood loss by the time I killed the fae."

"You killed a wild fae?" I asked, incredulous. "Those are some of the strongest fae in the world!"

"I cheated. I had salt in my pocket. The wild fae are like slugs—they hate salt." He shifted. "I threw it in his eyes, and he screamed. Then I choked him to death."

"So you escaped," I said slowly.

"I did," Charles said, sitting up straight. "And now you know one of the stories that only my commanding officer knows. We prettied it up for Santos's widow." He fell silent, staring out the window. "It's probably a good thing you never deployed," he said harshly. "You never want to see the things I did."

"I always felt guilty," I said, turning the wheel. "Like I wasn't a complete soldier."

He glanced at me. "You served," Charles said. He tapped out "Reveille" again. "You were willing to go. That's what matters."

I laughed. "There was a time when I wanted to be a female Ranger." I pulled into the parking lot of Franconi's. "We're here."

I started to get out, but Charles's hand caught mine. "Eileen," he said, voice serious. "You served. That's what matters." His eyes searched mine for a long moment before he released me. "Stay there," he ordered. I frowned, confused. Charles got out of the car and walked around, opening the driver's side door. "You," he said, "are a lady. And I am endeavoring to treat you as such."

I laughed. "A lady?" I said incredulously. "I am no such thing."

"I don't mean delicate and weak," Charles said. He struggled for a moment. "This means more to me than a fling," he said carefully. "I want to do this right."

I blinked. "Thank you," I said, touched.

"I meant what I said," Charles said, holding out his hand. I put my hand in his and smiled tremulously. His eyes lightened.

"I'm paying," he insisted as we walked into Franconi's. I just nodded with a sigh.

I had a large, black coffee with scone. Charles insisted on more coffee. As he insisted, he paid—but he didn't see the five-dollar bill I slipped into his briefcase. We sat in comfortable silence. I inhaled the scent of the coffee and bit into the crumbly scone. Heaven.

"Don't forget, we have another lesson tonight. And dinner."

I nodded, leaning back in my chair. "Of course," I said, flicking my fingers to get rid of crumbs. "And we still don't know who followed me last night."

Charles's eyes darkened. "We don't," he agreed. "I need to ask some people some questions." He brooded for a moment. "And, of course, you need your holster." I sighed. I'd left the pistol in the car.

"We'd better leave now," I said, standing, "or we won't make it to work on time." I checked my cell phone. It was eight thirty.

Charles stood fluidly and pressed something into my hand. I peered down at it. It was the five-dollar bill I'd slipped in his briefcase.

"Nice try," he said, smiling. He held out his hand. "Shall we go?"

I sighed, slipping my hand into his. "You let me buy dinner," I bargained.

"No way," he said. We walked to the car together, debating it.

Charles stopped dead. I looked up. A beautiful woman, clearly fae, was leaning against the car.

"Stay here, Eileen," Charles said, dropping my hand and starting forward.

"Not a chance," I said, walking along with him. "I punched Prince Faolain in the nose. I can do the same thing to her."

Charles glared at me, then focused again on the fae. "Don't—put too much stock in what she says," he said, voice tight. I frowned. Together, we walked up to the fae.

She was tall, with long black hair tossed carelessly over one shoulder. She wore a chic black dress, black leggings, and tall stiletto boots, emphasizing her slender frame. She was built, I noted with some envy, like a Parisian model. She watched us as we approached, preternaturally still.

"Charles," she said once we'd gotten into earshot. "And Ms. O'Donnell, of course." Her eyes flicked to me dismissively.

"Lady," Charles replied, bowing shallowly at the waist.

"Now, Charles," she scolded, "once you did better than that." Her eyes flashed. "Call me by my name."

"We no longer have that type of relationship, my lady." Charles refused to look at me, but his hand squeezed mine. I fought to keep the surprise off my face. A relationship? Between a human and a fae? What was going on?

"You mean," the fae murmured softly, danger-
ously, "you chose to no longer have that type of
relationship with me." Her eyes flashed again, and
she looked to me, a small sneer marring her perfect
face. "He'll treat you like a princess," she warned me,
"have your legs over your head, and then dump you
like yesterday's trash."

I kept my head high. "I beg your pardon," I said
frigidly, "but I don't know you."

The fae laughed bitterly. "I am Severine de
Bough, of Western Wind." She smiled at me, taunting. "Don't let the face fool you. I'm only part fae;
my father, the king, in his goodwill, raised me as
part of his kingdom."

"My lady," Charles cut in, "he uses you most
abominably."

Her eyes cut to him, going hard. "Like you'd
know," she snapped. "Don't project your own—fail-
ures—onto me, Charles." She smirked at me. "From
the look on your face, I take it he hasn't told you."

"Like I said, I don't know you," I said, feeling
the grip on my hand harden. "Why should I trust
anything you say?"

Severine threw her head back and laughed, a
sparkling sound that could've brought the birds
from the trees. "Oh, you're good," she taunted.
"You'd last at court, absolutely, no question." She
smiled brittlely. "It'd be far crueler to let you find
out for yourself," she said, eyeing me with satisfac-

tion. She gracefully stood, patting my car as she did. "You're slipping, Charles," Severine said, pointing at him.

Charles made no reply but narrowed his eyes, staring at her stonily. Severine smiled seraphically. "I'm sure I'll see you around." She snapped her fingers. I blinked, and she was gone.

"Let's go," Charles said, grip still tight on my hand. "We need to leave."

"Did you know her?" I asked, as he walked me to the car.

"Unfortunately, yes," he said grimly. He looked at me and sighed, then held open the car door for me as I unlocked it.

"Severine is half-human, half-fae," he explained. "She's the daughter of the king of Western Wind by one of his slaves." He paused. "She looks more fae than human, which saved her from the fate of her sisters and brothers. She was brought up in the king's home, as his daughter."

I frowned. "But how do you know her?"

He shut the car door and walked around to the passenger door, opening it and sliding in. "Severine left the court for a short time," he said shortly. "I met her at a bar where she was slumming. She was attracted to me for the rebellion. I was attracted to her for the forbidden." Charles shrugged.

"She still sounds pretty bitter," I said, pulling out of the parking lot and carefully steering into the street.

"She may be," Charles said, "because I left her, and she didn't leave me."

I kept quiet. It had seemed to be more than that.

"You know this is different, right?" His voice was low, earnest. "She was nothing to me."

I nodded noncommittally.

"I'm dead serious, Eileen," Charles insisted. "You're special."

"I don't understand a few things," I admitted.

He looked at me cautiously. "And what are those?"

I held a finger up. "First," I said, "why she was there in the first place. Second," I held a second finger up, "why you're interested in me at all. And third," I held up a third finger, "Charles, you're a hound dog. Everybody says so. Why should this time be any different?"

Charles went quiet for a moment. "In order of importance," he said, voice a growl, "First, it was probably Western Wind following us last night. And Severine could never control herself; she just gave us a warning and a clue." He reached over and grabbed my hand. "Second, you're beautiful, you're smart, you're strong. Why shouldn't I be interested?" The pressure on my hand increased. "And third," he said, voice dropping even lower, "this time is different. I've never felt this way before."

I shrugged helplessly. "Charles," I said, "We've known each other for three weeks. Most of that's been through work. How in the name of the Lady of the Lake do you know how you feel?"

"I know how I feel," he said obstinately. "And I'd like to point out I've talked more about my emotions in the past twenty-four hours than I have in my entire thirty-three years on earth." He frowned. "It's not natural." I glanced at him. "Eyes on the road," Charles snapped.

My eyes snapped back before I realized what he'd said. "I can drive," I said, coldly furious.

"I know you can," he said, voice going soft. "But I also don't want you to die in a fiery crash because you're glaring at me." There was a note of laughter in his voice.

"Why would Western Wind be following me?" I asked, going for the easiest revelation.

"My guess," Charles said, voice cold, "is it's because of your bond with Faolain."

CHAPTER 7

"IT WOULD BE a tactical advantage," I agreed, "to have someone who could listen to Faolain's mind." A shiver rippled down my spine.

"It's more than that, Eileen." Charles looked at me gravely. "Faolain probably didn't tell you, but you can't kill someone in a bond without also killing the other person." He picked up my hand and squeezed it. "Kill you, kill Faolain."

I swallowed. "The second fae said something like that," I said, my voice small. "The day of our fight."

"What did the second fae look like?" Charles's voice went sharp.

I searched my memory. The second fae had been eminently forgettable, compared to Faolain. "He looked a lot like Faolain," I said after a moment. "Like they could've been brothers."

Charles leaned back with a sigh. "Eamon," he said, voice bitter.

"Who's Eamon?"

"Faolain's half-brother. Another half-human, half-fae who inherited the fae side of the genetic balance." He glanced at me. "Eamon is bad news. He's usually tasked to assist Faolain with hunting down escaped slaves, and there's some rumor that he serves as the spymaster for Northern Sun."

"They give a half-human that much power?"

"He earned it." Charles leaned forward and stared out the window. "He's brutal," he said, voice low. "Absolutely detests humans—they're reminders of his, quote, weakness, unquote." Charles looked at me. "He didn't intervene in the fight at all?"

"No," I said slowly. "It was between me and Faolain."

"Interesting," Charles said. "Normally it would've been his fight, not Faolain's. It's his job to get in between his prince and possible danger."

Charles brooded for the rest of the drive. When we got to the NVRA, he said in a tone that brooked no arguments, "We are going to a gun store for that holster at lunch today."

I nodded, patting the gun. I'd slid it into my waistband but could hear the screams of my old instructors echoing in my head. *You're going to blow your ass off!*

I got out of the car. Charles was still sitting in the passenger seat. He pulled out his phone and began to text. "Wait a moment," he said distractedly. He finished texting and got out of the car as well, rounding the car in long strides to meet up with me. "Ready?" he asked.

"Let's go."

Jenny, Anna, and Garrett were standing in the War Room, clustered around Anna's cell phone. Anna looked up. "Good morning, Charles, Eileen," she said. She glanced at me. "I understand you had a run-in with Severine de Bough."

I nodded. "I wouldn't call it a run-in. More that she appeared, threw a few cryptic sentences, and then disappeared."

Anna sighed. "Sounds like Severine de Bough to a T," she remarked. She pulled out a folder and handed it to me. "We just finished updating her dossier with the contact information."

I frowned. "You call that contact? She chatted for a minute and left."

Jenny gave a nasty laugh. Charles placed a hand protectively at the small of my back. Garrett looked stony.

"Well," Anna said, "she is Charles's ex-girlfriend. And she is from Western Wind. She has reason to have an interest in you."

"Charles has a lot of ex-girlfriends," Jenny put in sweetly. She gazed at him, eyebrows raised. He ignored her, expression cool.

Lot of ex-girlfriends lot of ex-girlfriends lot of ex-girlfriends, Joe chanted in my head. I made a face, shaking my head violently. Charles looked at me carefully.

"Are you all right?"

"Yes," I said shortly. "Just fine." I changed the

subject. "So what's on the agenda for today?"

"Mission briefing," Anna said cheerfully. "We've assigned Strike Team 3 to the mission to Northern Sun. The medic team has been hanging out in Vermont for four days ... it's time to move."

Charles frowned. "Strike Team 3 just went on a mission, Anna. Send someone else."

She looked regretful. "Unfortunately, Charles, we don't have anyone else capable of carrying out this mission." She waved us all to the table. Charles sat, his lips compressed in a thin line.

"Here's the operations order. Jenny just finished writing it." She slid it across the table to Charles. He picked it up and read it, lips puckered. "I'm not comfortable with leaving Eileen right now," he said abruptly.

"We can protect her," Garrett rumbled.

"I can also protect myself," I interjected

Charles snorted. "You may have driven Faolain off once, but he'll be ready for a physical attack next time." He lowered the operations order. "He knows you have no magic."

"I do, however, have a pistol."

He snorted again. "Best case, that'll give you time to run." He gave me a grim look.

"Look," I said. "I have a group of people around me. You, however, are needed to smuggle some poor human out of fae territory. You are the only one who can do that." I paused. "I'll be fine. You go do your thing."

He looked at me, long and level, lips compressed in a grim line. "Fine," he bit out. "But you'd better still be here when I get back."

"I have absolutely no intention of leaving."

"Back to the operation," Anna interjected. "You'll leave here tomorrow, 0400. You'll travel straight to Northern Sun, reach it no later than two days from now, and rendezvous with the target." She consulted her notes. "This is a couple, a man and a woman. Both approximately eighteen years of age, reportedly in good health. You'll take them to the Vermont safe house, with radio check-ins at base twice a day, using our secure channel. Meet up with Phillip before you leave to confirm the radios are synced magically." She paused. "Any questions?"

"No," Charles said, reading through the operations order, forehead creased. "I'll brief my team tonight at 1600 hours."

"Excellent." Anna stood, shoving her papers back in her briefcase. "The operations order is blood-locked, so you can take it outside of the building."

Charles nodded absently. "I'll need a computer in here," he said.

"Of course." Anna waved her hand. "Take any but the BFT system."

He nodded, picked up the operations order without another word, and sat down at a computer. He looked deep in thought.

I felt a sudden sense of loss at the thought of Charles not being around for the next week. He'd become a fixture in my life. I frowned at the thought. Had he really? We'd known each other for only a few weeks. felt a fission of fear go down my spine at the thought of him walking into Northern Sun.

Relax, I told myself firmly. *He's done this before. He'll be fine.*

NorthernSunNorthernSunNORTHERNSUN, Sheldon chanted in my head. I shook my head sharply to dislodge him.

"All right, Eileen?" I looked up. Garrett was scrutinizing me.

I smiled weakly. "I'm fine," I said, perhaps a bit too quickly. Garrett noticed, by the way his eyes narrowed. Before he could continue to probe me, however, Anna looked up.

"Okay," she said, clapping her hands. "We have our last mission of the season to plan for." She unrolled her map. "This is to the Kingdom of Texas, and we'll be coordinating with another rescue association, since it's so far away. The North Carolina Rescue Association." Anna pointed at me. "You have a conference call with their assistant director today at one."

I nodded, thrilled. They were beginning to give me more responsibility. "I'll be there," I promised.

Anna nodded back. "Excellent. Let's get started."

We mission planned for the next five hours, not breaking for lunch. At around ten, Charles left, muttering about needing to check his gear. "And you'll do a PCC/PCI for your team," Garrett said firmly.

Charles looked at him with exasperation. "Don't I always check my team's gear before we roll out?" The tension in the air deepened for a moment.

"All right," Anna said, breaking it. "I'll see you later, Charles."

"Four o'clock," he promised. He walked over to me, lifted my hand, and pressed a kiss into my palm. "Tie a yellow ribbon round the old oak tree," he said, half laughing.

I swallowed and stood up. Grabbing his shoulders, I lifted myself up and kissed him gently on the mouth. He blinked.

"Come home quick," I said, my voice husky. Charles nodded, eyes wide. Of all the kisses we'd shared, that had been the first one I'd initiated.

"I will," he murmured, voice deep. He grabbed my shoulders and kissed me again, deep and long.

"All right, lovebirds." Garrett's voice sounded behind us. "You're putting on a show. Time to get back to work."

We broke apart, gasping. Charles seized my hand. "You be careful," he whispered. "I won't be able to help you, where I'm at."

"I will be," I promised.

He held my eyes, looking deep into them. Finally, he broke my gaze. "All right," he said hoarsely. "Time to go." With one last look at me, he walked out of the War Room.

"All right," Anna said, looking both amused and sad. "Eileen, you have that conference call in three hours, don't forget."

"I haven't," I said, turning around.

"All right. Let's get back to work." She consulted her papers. "We still need to look at these scout reports for one of the routes to the Kingdom of Texas. Get a map, Jenny."

The next three hours dragged. I couldn't stop thinking of Charles and his mission. I had a bad feeling. *It's nothing*, I told myself. *Don't worry about it*. I focused back on my papers, squinting fiercely.

"All right, then, Eileen," Anna's voice broke in. "Time for your conference call." I was already up and headed toward the computer. I logged in and opened Skype. The screen revealed a man's face.

"This is the North Carolina Rescue Association. I'm Ellis," he greeted me. "We're on a secure line here."

"I'm Eileen, Northern Virginia Rescue Association. We're on a secure line here, too."

"Awesome, Eileen. Shall we begin? We're looking at this mission to the Kingdom of Texas next week, correct?"

"Absolutely," I replied. "How many missions do you run?"

"We normally run smaller-scale missions, mostly into the south of Western Wind. We don't usually touch the Kingdom of Texas. But," he consulted a piece of paper on his desk, "we've received valuable intel from the rebels in the kingdom. The queen, Siobhan, is going to be in Washington, DC next week, at her embassy. It's the perfect time to strike."

I nodded. "Do you have any intel on the people we're picking up?"

He shook his head. "Just a meeting place." Ellis consulted his notes again. "Grid coordinates 78681013, 89241810. It's the top of a small hill right outside the border of the queen's estate."

I frowned. "That's going to be difficult, tactically," I said slowly. "Top of a hill? The risk of silhouetting is very high. My team will be low crawling all the way up and down the hill. Is there any other place they can meet?"

Ellis shook his head. "Unfortunately not—those were the only coordinates provided by the rebels, and they've gone silent. We can't raise them."

I frowned. "That sounds ominous."

"It's not unusual," he assured me. "Sometimes they have to move quickly, to avoid the fae hunters. They're really trying to crack down on the rebels now." He looked sad.

We talked for about an hour longer, going over three potential routes into the Kingdom of Texas. "I'll send you the maps," Ellis promised. "And you can pick the rendezvous points for our teams." I nodded, pleased.

After he signed off, I leaned back with a sigh. I looked down at my sheet of notes and waved Anna over. "Here's what I got from the call," I said, handing her the sheet. She barely looked at it before thrusting it back to me.

"Great," she said. "Type them up as a WARNO and get it to me by tomorrow evening." I nodded, pleased. Being trusted to type up a warning order, the first step in activating a mission, was a huge sign of trust.

Garrett waved me over to where he sat at the table. "All right, Eileen," he grunted. "Let's go over personnel requirements for this mission." He frowned. "We could send Strike Team 3—"

"But they will have already been on a mission this week" I objected.

Garrett looked at me sharply. "Exactly what I was going to say," he agreed. "Maybe Strike Team 7. They haven't been out for a month, and they're good enough to get down to the Kingdom of Texas with minimal problems." He paused. "We'll also need someone at the North Carolina Rescue Association to coordinate."

"I can go," I said quickly.

"No, we need you here, to run the op from this side." Garrett frowned. "We could send Rima," he said. "She's an experienced coordinator."

"All right, Rima it is."

We talked for another hour before he let me go. "You'll need to alert the Strike Team 7 team leader as soon as you get that WARNO done," Garrett said gruffly.

"I know," I said, patience wearing thin.

Garrett laughed. "I haven't forgotten your training, Eileen. But I'm an old sergeant first class. My job is to check lieutenants." His eyes twinkled merrily at me. I sighed and laughed.

"You might as well go home, Eileen," Anna said from the other side of the room. "You've done all your work for today, and you'll be here late enough later. Get some rest while you can."

I nodded. "Thanks, Anna. And thanks, Garrett," I added, looking over at him. He nodded, raising a hand, and Anna smiled.

"And I know that Charles wanted you to get a holster for your pistol," she added. Her eyes flickered down to where the pistol was still stashed in my waistband. I grinned.

"Yeah, I should go do that," I said, raising my hand in farewell. I jogged outside. I glanced at my cell phone. Three o'clock. Charles would be holding his briefing for his team in an hour.

My phone buzzed. There was a text from an unknown number. I opened it, frowning.

"Hey beautiful. I'm thinking of you."

My heart started to beat faster. "Who is this?"

I texted back.

"Charles."

My heart slowed. "How did you get my number?"

There was a minute's delay before the response came in. "I have intelligence assets everywhere."

I laughed. "Do they begin and end with A?"

"I'll never give up my sources."

I sighed. "I'll miss you," I typed, and then paused, my finger hovering over the send button. I compressed my lips and resolutely hit it.

"I'll miss you too, beautiful."

I smiled softly and unlocked my car. My phone buzzed again.

"Now go buy yourself a holster."

I laughed, slightly hysterically, and pulled out of the parking lot.

I stopped by the gun store and bought a holster, lingering to look at the accessories. I just didn't want to go home, I thought, and face having to think about Charles. I bought myself Chinese and sat in one of the booths, idly people watching. My phone buzzed again. Smiling, I looked down at it.

"You're making a mistake."

I frowned. "Who is this?" I texted back

"A friend. You shouldn't trust Charles Talbot. He keeps secrets."

"Like what?" I asked. I waited, but there was no reply.

Rattled, I gathered up my tray and threw away my trash. I walked outside, looking carefully through the parking lot. There was no one standing out or looking suspicious. I jogged to my car, keys at the ready, and locked myself in. I pulled out my cell phone again and texted Charles.

"You okay?" I waited, but there was no response. I pulled out of the parking space, driving home as quickly as I could. There was no one there.

I went up to my room, shivering slightly. I could feel the adrenaline rushing, needing to do something. I checked my cell phone. I had just enough time to make it to Muay Thai. I changed into my boxing shorts and a tank top and pulled my hair back into a ponytail. Grabbing my bag of gear, I headed out to my car.

I made it to Muay Thai with just under five minutes to spare. The coach, Dominic, looked up at me when I walked into the gym. He raised an eyebrow. "Been a few weeks," he commented.

I shrugged. "I ran out of money, got a job, lost a job, got another job ... you know how it goes."

"Oh?" He raised an eyebrow. "Where are you working?"

"The Northern Virginia Rescue Association," I replied, a little nervous. It was a controversial topic, especially with the sanctuary law under fire.

"That's awesome," he said, impressed. "You're doing good work."

"Thanks," I said with a smile. I dropped my bag on a bench. "Not many people here tonight."

"Not really," he agreed, "but we'll have enough." He waved his hand. "Let's go. It's time."

I walked out into the center of the gym, where five men already waited. I knew most of them— Tom, Hayashi, Jerry, and Ivan were already warming up, swinging kicks at punching bags. The fifth man was punching the bag, his face sweaty. I stared at him. He wasn't wearing a shirt, only boxing shorts; I could see his muscled physique from the other side of the gym. I blushed, thinking of Charles.

Time to work, I told myself sternly. I wrapped my hands, careful to bind up the knuckles. Dominic clapped his hands. "Let's start," he said loudly. "Everyone grab a jump rope. Every time you trip over the rope, ten pushups." He set the timer, grinning evilly.

I did a lot of pushups. The new man, who hadn't been introduced, didn't do any. Several times I felt his eyes lingering on me and fought the urge to draw into myself. I had every right to be here, I told myself firmly, and he was probably just surprised to see a woman in the otherwise all-male class.

We split into partners for drills, and I found myself partnered with the new man. He smiled at me, a quick quirk of his lips. "What's your name?" he asked.

"Eileen," I said shortly, readjusting my hand wraps and putting the boxing gloves on over them.

"Eileen." The name seemed to run off his tongue. "Pleasure. I'm Will." He stuck out his hand to shake. I looked at him, then at the gloves I'd just put on, and bumped his hand with my fist instead. He laughed.

"All right, Eileen. Let's go." He threw a punch at my head. I wove, remembering how Faolain had sent a lancet of flame at my head. "You're fast," Will said with pleased surprise. He jabbed at my stomach. I blocked it. We settled into a comfortable rhythm, sending jabs back and forth.

"So tell me, Eileen, what brings you to Muay Thai?"

I shrugged, jabbing at his face. He blocked it. "I like the exercise."

"And I bet it's good self-defense," Will added, lips quirking again.

I nodded. "Sure it is. Why are you here?" I challenged.

"Same reasons," he said with a shrug. "And one other." He leaned in, and his eyes suddenly turned black. I jumped back, landing in a fighting crouch.

"We are watching you," he said, his voice suddenly a much deeper timber, "Be careful, Eileen O'Donnell. You don't know what you're playing with." He suddenly kicked, catching me right above the knee. I winced but kept my guard up, looking for an opening. His hands were up next to his face and he bobbed from foot to foot, smirking wickedly.

"Your Charles isn't here," he continued, "and there's no one to save you. What would you do if I—just—took—you—away?" He jabbed with each word, the jabs coming faster and faster. I was barely avoiding them at this point. Finally, I got a kick in, right at his stomach. He gasped, bending over slightly, but not low enough for me to grab his neck.

"I'm not that easy a target," I muttered, looking for another opening. I jabbed at him and followed up with a kick. He avoided both and laughed.

"Eileen, you're *such* an easy target. Even with Charles there, we could've taken you any time we wanted to. No," he continued, smirking, "this is a polite warning. Stay away from Prince Faolain. And"—he leaned in to whisper—"it might be in your best interest to avoid Charles Talbot, as well." My next punch got him right on the eye.

"What's going on?" Dominic asked from behind me. "This is drilling, not sparring."

"Sorry," I said, voice cool. "Total mistake."

"Sorry," Will echoed. He stepped back, stripping off his boxing gloves. "I think I'm done for tonight." He nodded to me. "Remember what I said." He strode off, sweat glistening in the gym's fluorescent lights.

"What just happened?" Dominic asked after a moment. He frowned at me.

I shrugged. "Just an asshole," I said, willing my pulse to calm. "Who can I drill with now?"

"I'll drill with you," Dominic said slowly. "But are you sure you're all right?"

"I'm totally fine," I lied. "Let's go. I've already wasted enough time on that jackass."

The rest of the lesson passed quickly, and I grabbed my bag and sweatshirt from the bench, pulling my sweatshirt on with relief. I frowned, thinking, and pulled out my cell phone, fingers poised to make a phone call. I couldn't call Charles— he was hopefully asleep and getting ready for the mission tomorrow. I called Anna instead. The phone went to voicemail. I sighed and called Garrett.

"What's wrong, Eileen?" He sounded alert.

"I just had a really weird run-in." I told him about Will and the threats he'd made.

"You said his name was Will?"

"Yes."

"Did he look human, or fae?"

"He looked human, but his eyes turned black when he talked to me."

Garrett sounded even more alert. "His eyes turned black?"

"Yes." I suppressed a shiver. "They did."

"Okay. That narrows it down some. Sounds like a half-human, half-fae. But we don't have a dossier on anyone named Will, working for either Western Wind or Northern Sun." He paused again. "Come back to the office. I want you to sleep here tonight. Have you told Charles?"

"No!" I said, shocked. "He needs to be ready for his mission tomorrow."

"Yes. Yes he does." Garrett went silent. "Okay," he said after a moment, "I won't tell him either. But you need to get your ass in here. Understood?"

"Understood," I said, unlocking my car door and sliding in.

"Eileen," Garrett said with a sigh, "please tell me you were locked in your car when you made this call."

"No," I admitted, "I was walking across the parking lot."

"We'll discuss personal safety measures later," he snapped. "But if someone is threatening to grab you, don't walk across the parking lot on your cell phone. It's distracting. Stay alert, stay alive."

"Hooah, Sergeant."

"And don't get sassy with me either, Lieutenant. You get in here. Now." Garrett hung up.

I drove to the NVRA in silence, not wanting to turn on my radio for fear of distraction. What if they rammed my car? I suppressed a shiver. But who, I wondered, was Will—and what did he want? It seemed like more players were entering the game every day.

I pulled into the NVRA parking lot. Garrett was waiting for me outside. "Let's go," he said tightly, escorting me through the door. I sighed, missing Charles. We walked in silence to the War Room. Anna was sitting there, looking worried.

"A man with eyes that turned black, hmm?" she asked me as I walked in. "Are you all right?"

"I'm fine," I assured her. "But I don't know what that was all about."

"He could've been working for Western Wind," Garrett said. "But they wouldn't want you to stay away from Faolain or Charles. You make them vulnerable."

"So they must've been working for Northern Sun," I said slowly. "But why would they want me to stay away from Charles? That makes no sense."

"None of it does," Anna said grimly. She pushed a stack of folders over to me. "These are all the operatives we know of from Northern Sun and Western Wind. I want you to look through them and see if anyone looks familiar."

I went through file after file. Fae face after fae face stared out at me. "None of these look familiar," I said, thumping the last one closed. "I told you, he looked human."

Anna and Garrett exchanged glances. "Well," Anna said matter-of-factly, "I guess we have a mystery then." She took back the stack of file folders. "You will be sleeping here until this is all cleared up. You should probably text your family and let them know."

I got out my cell phone. "Do you think they're safe?" I asked, busily texting.

"We have a strike team on them," Anna said. "Charles insisted." Her eyes danced for a moment.

"Though I don't know whether that was to provide you with a chaperone, protect your family, or both."

I swallowed. "Thank you," I said sincerely. "I know that's terribly expensive."

"We just won't get our SINCGARS radio for a few more months," Anna said with a wave of her hand. "Do you feel comfortable sleeping in the conference room?"

"Yes," I said, "but do you have anything to sleep on?"

Anna smiled. "You're not the first to be threatened," she said. "We have a whole closet of sleeping bags in the conference room. If it gets worse, though, we're going to have to come up with alternative arrangements. Probably one of our safe houses."

"I'm sure this will be fine," I said hurriedly.

"Do you have your medication?" Garrett interjected.

"I always carry it with me." I held up my bottle of Clozaril for inspection.

"Good." He led me to the conference room and opened a closet door, pulling out a sleeping bag and sleeping pad. "No pillows—sorry. We had to wash them after our last refugee had lice," he explained.

"Lice," I said faintly. "Yeah, I'll skip that." I dragged the sleeping bag over to the corner and put the pad down, spreading the sleeping bag out over it.

"Okay, Eileen. Sleep well. The next shift will be here soon, and Anna and I will be leaving."

I blinked sleepily. "Who's on it?"

"Jenny and Rima," he said. "Then Lia might be in as well. But for now, sleep." Garrett left the room, closing the door after him.

I sighed and lay down in the sleeping bag. I'd forgotten a charging cord for my cell phone, so I turned it off. I curled up and fell asleep.

I awoke the next morning with a horrible migraine. I groaned, rolling over; there was no relief.

"That's what happens when you skip your coffee." Joe knelt next to my sleeping bag, staring at me.

I froze, staring at him. I'd forgotten to take my medication last night. Quickly, I pawed through my purse, grabbing the Clozaril and dry-swallowing.

"It's too late for that." Sheldon appeared next to Joe in a sparkle of gold. "You know what happens when you forget your medication."

"Yeah," Joe said with a smirk. "We're here. All day."

"We're your curse," Sheldon said in a sing-song voice. "We'll never leave. Never, ever, ever."

I gazed at them both. My diseased mind had produced Sheldon and Joe both as tall, fit men, six foot five and dark. Joe was dressed in an army uniform with a captain's rank. Sheldon was wearing a rumpled suit.

"Go away," I snapped, holding my hand to my head. "I don't have time for this."

"You can't ignore us," Joe pointed out. "We're here to stay."

I stood, fumbling my way to the War Room. "Griffin," I hissed at it. The door opened.

Rima and Jenny were still there, both staring at the BFT. "Morning," Rima said without looking up. "There's a coffee pot over there." She waved her hand in the direction of a small cabinet. I stumbled over and found a coffee pot, coffee, and filters shoved inside. "Bless you," I said fervently, getting all the supplies out.

Rima nodded distractedly. "What do you make of this?" she asked Jenny, pointing at the BFT. Curious, I came closer. Three dots were pulsing on the screen. As I watched, a fourth dot appeared, then disappeared.

"Probably just a bogey," Jenny said dismissively. She glanced at me. "This is your boyfriend's mission," she said with a slight sneer.

I ignored it. "How are they doing?" I asked eagerly.

"Well enough," she said shortly. "They crossed the border into the boundary area this morning at seven o'clock. They haven't made contact with the target yet."

I nodded, swallowing. The coffee machine beeped. I picked up the pot and poured into a Styrofoam cup I found on the other side of the file cabinet. It looked a little dirty, I thought, eyeing it, but it was the only cup I could find. I looked at the BFT again. The fourth dot appeared, then disappeared. I frowned.

"Are we sure that's just an anomaly?" I asked.

Rima opened her mouth to answer, but Jenny wheeled to me. "Look, Eileen," she said, eyes flashing, "I'm the one in charge right now. I get that you're some kind of wunderkind—at least that's what Anna says—but you know what I think? I think you're just a very sick woman who needs to be out of here. You're a liability."

I stared at her, my mouth open. "Okay then," I said, when my voice felt strong enough to speak. I pointed at the BFT. "But you didn't answer my question."

Jenny flushed a brilliant red. "Yes," she said, voice tight. "I'm certain that's just an anomaly. Probably the equipment acting up."

"Boss," Rima said, voice taut. She pointed at the BFT. A fifth—a sixth—a seventh dot appeared out of nowhere.

Jenny stared. "Do a radio check," she instructed. Rima nodded, reaching for the radio.

"Charlie Tango, this is base, over."

The radio remained silent.

"Charlie Tango, this is base, over."

Still no answer.

I felt my heart rate pick up speed.

"Oh, there it goes," Sheldon said sympathetically from behind me. "Here's the disaster. This is why you can't have nice things, Eileen."

I whirled around. "Shut up!"

"Excuse me?" Jenny looked up, eyes hard.

"Not you," I snapped. I stepped closer to the BFT. The three dots that had just appeared were so close to Charles and his team they appeared to be touching. "A Sending," I said suddenly. "You need to do a Sending."

"Oh," Jenny said sarcastically, "and a cloud of glittery blue appearing in the air won't be indiscreet at all." She nailed me with another hard glance.

Frantically, I reached for my cell phone. It was still off. I turned it on and got the beep of incoming messages. One was from my mother. One was from Nate. And one—my breath caught—was Charles. I opened it.

"Good morning, beautiful. See you soon."

"Charles! Answer me! You're about to be ambushed!" I texted back.

Rima gasped. I looked up. The BFT had gone completely black. Jenny swore. In another second, it turned back on, but all the dots were gone.

"What happened?" Jenny demanded.

"I don't know!" Rima's fingers were dancing across the keyboard. "They're just—gone. I can't reestablish contact."

Jenny grabbed the radio. "Charlie Tango, this is base. Come in. Over."

The radio hissed with static. I flinched. It sounded like laughter. Jenny dropped the radio.

"What's going on?" Anna walked into the War Room. "Jenny, I just got your message."

"The team's gone off the BFT," I said, jabbing my finger at it, "and we can't raise them on radio."

"Thank you, Eileen," Jenny said acidly. "It's pretty much what she just said, Anna," she said. "We can't raise them."

Anna frowned. "How far away is the secondary team?"

"That's Strike Force 1," Rima reported. "I'm calling them up now."

"Scouting mission only," Anna ordered. "I'm not sending more people into a disaster. Tell them it's radio contact every fifteen minutes."

"Roger." Rima didn't look up from her keyboard.

"One more thing, Anna," Jenny said, pointing at me. "She didn't take her medication last night."

Anna didn't look up. "Is that really important right now, Jenny?"

Jenny flushed red. "She's been shouting at the walls," she said angrily. "It's distracting."

Anna sighed. "Eileen, get out," she said. "Don't leave the conference room. Come back when you're stable." She walked over to the radio.

"But—"

"Go." She didn't look up. "I'll keep you updated on the team," she said more gently.

Fighting back tears, I let myself out of the War Room and collapsed again on my sleeping bag in the conference room. I pulled out my cell phone. I was down to ten percent, I noticed. Suddenly I blinked. Charles was typing.

My phone buzzed. "Do you want your boy-friend alive?"

My phone chimed again. Trembling, I looked at the next message. It was a picture of Charles in a cell, unconscious, bloody.

I stood up, ready to go to Anna.

"Don't tell anyone about this. We'll know, and we'll kill him." I sat back down with a thump.

"That's better. If you want him alive, turn off your phone, drive to the embassy, and tell Faolain that you're ready. And leave your pistol in the car."

"Ready for what?" I typed back.

My phone buzzed. "No more questions. Do it, or Charles Talbot dies."

Shaking, I turned off my cell phone and stowed it in my purse.

"There she goes," Joe murmured from behind me. "Off to meet the wizard."

"The wonderful wizard of Oz," Sheldon agreed with a snicker.

Ignoring them both, I made my way to the door, opening it gingerly. No one was there. Slipping out, I jogged through the parking lot and unlocked my car. Slamming the door, I skidded out of the parking lot, fishtailing into the road. Words flashed in front of my dashboard.

"We're still watching. Don't get in an accident, now."

"Screw you," I muttered through clenched teeth.

"Language! Is that any way for a lady to speak?"

I ignored it. Joe and Sheldon were in the back seat, singing. Their twin tenor voices rose together in a beautiful Latin chant. I swallowed. I recognized the lament for the dead.

It took me thirty minutes to drive to the embassy, and every minute weighed on me. I parked the car in the driveway, remembering Charles's comment about losing my escape route. I stormed up the stairs, ignoring the valet as he came to take my keys. As I passed him, I could've sworn I saw a smile flicker across his lips.

I pounded on the door. The same fae as before opened it, raising his eyebrows in surprise.

"I'm here for Prince Faolain," I said shortly. My breath came from me in great gasps, as though I'd run a hundred miles.

"I will check and see if he is available. May I tell him what this is about?"

I laughed bitterly. "He knows. Tell him that. And tell him I'm ready."

For the first time, the fae gave a shallow bow. "As you wish," he murmured.

CHAPTER 8

───⟡───

IT TOOK ALMOST ten minutes for Faolain to emerge. This time, instead of the small room to the right, he gestured me up the stairs. "Come," he said shortly.

"I'm not a dog," I snapped, following him. A grim smile touched his lips, but he said nothing.

He led me to a grand room at the top of the stairs. It was dominated by a four-poster bed, draped in a canopy of scarlet silk. A small table sat to one side of the room, surrounded by four wooden chairs. A giant oak dresser stood next to the bed. Other than that, the room was bare. Faolain stopped and gestured me to one of the chairs. I hesitated.

"If you prefer," he said, his eyes raking over me, "we could move this to the bed."

"No thanks," I snapped, pulling out a chair with a jerk. I sat, staring at Faolain with challenge in my eyes. He looked back, that same grim smile on his face.

"So spirited," he remarked. He gracefully drew out a chair and sat. "Now. You're ready?"

I shrugged. "I want my boyfriend alive."

"I see." He was laughing at me, though no sign of it showed on his face.

"You realize," he said, voice soft, "that you came here with no guarantee of safe passage. No guarantee of safe treatment. No guarantees at all. None."

I looked back at him stonily.

"Such devotion," Faolain murmured. He reached over and gently touched my cheek. "Would that Charles Talbot was worthy of it."

"I decide whether he's worthy of it or not," I snapped. "I want him back."

Faolain leaned back in his chair, throwing one hand gracefully over the back. "Why don't you text Charles Talbot's captors and see what they want you to do next."

"Don't play games with me!" I stood, knocking the chair over. It fell to the ground with a thud. "You're the prince of Northern Sun. You tell them to let him go!"

"Alas," Faolain said softly, "my father's regime has not been terribly stable of late." He smirked. "Pretenders to the throne. They try to undercut him—and me—at every opportunity."

I swallowed. "So you don't have him," I said, beginning to understand. I stared at the cell phone in my hand. "So if they don't support you, why did they send me to you?" I asked angrily.

Faolain sighed. "I expect that they're going to

kill all three of us and frame you as a spy. To protect their real spy."

I blinked. "Wait—what?"

"Surely you don't think that humans can't be corrupted," he hissed silkily. He stood up, smirking. "Who is jealous enough, angry enough, at Charles Talbot and you to have you killed?"

"Jenny," I whispered angrily. "The bitch is dead."

He raised one finger warningly. "There is one small problem. First, someone wants all three of us dead. Second," his eyes flashed and his nostrils flared, "what makes you think I'll let you go if we survive?"

I stared at him, swallowing. I could feel a thick ball in the back of my throat.

"Not to worry," Faolain reassured me. "You won't be a servant. What I have planned for you is much ... more ... pleasurable." His nostrils flared again, and I stumbled back, horrified.

"Shocked into silence, are we?" Faolain took a step toward me. I retreated a step. "So that's all it takes," he murmured. "Good to know."

I scrambled to recover myself. "I defeated you once," I snapped. "I can do it again."

"My dear." He smiled sympathetically. "I am at the seat of my power, here. Do you truly think I can be defeated by a few punches and kicks?" I felt my feet fasten to the floor. Desperate, I tried to move them. They were stuck fast.

"You're in trooublllle," Joe and Sheldon sang from behind me.

Faolain approached me slowly, deliberately, his eyes flicking up and down my body. "That's better. Now," he said reaching up and tracing my face, "let's see what we have." He reached for my shirt.

I leaned away, as far as I could with my feet pasted to the floor. He chuckled. "None of that, now," he said admonishingly. "Don't worry. You might even enjoy it." He grasped my shirt, trying to pull me back.

I grabbed my chair and hit him.

His eyes went wide, and he staggered back before collapsing on the floor. My feet suddenly came free. I sighed in relief, straightening up and pulling my shirt down. I felt dirty.

"Dirty, dirty, dirty, dirty," Joe and Sheldon chanted behind me.

"Shut up," I snapped. I looked at Faolain, unconscious on the floor, and felt like crying. What was I supposed to do now? I was no closer to saving Charles, and maybe now in even worse trouble. I'd knocked out a fae prince in his own embassy. I had no idea what the law was, but I couldn't imagine it would end well.

A throat cleared at the door. "Well now," it said, deep and low, just like Faolain's. "You're in some trouble, aren't you?"

I jumped, whirling around. The second fae

from McConnell Consultants stood there, looking amused. "Eamon of Northern Sun," he said, bowing elegantly, one hand over his heart. "I believe you all at the Northern Virginia Rescue Association know me." His eyes flickered, still amused.

I drew myself up. "Yes. We do. Aren't you half-human? How do you justify hunting down your own kind?"

"Is this really the time to be asking me?" Eamon asked mildly. He gestured at Faolain on the floor. "You have very little time before he wakes up."

"What do you want?" I asked, feeling defeated.

Eamon's eyes glistened. "What if I told you that I could not only break your bond with Prince Faolain, but return your ... boyfriend ... to you, Eileen?"

"What do I have to do?" I tried to keep the eagerness out of my voice.

"It's quite simple, Eileen," he said with a smile. "Bond with *me*."

I blinked. "What?"

"Allow me to transfer the bond, from my prince"—he kicked lightly at Faolain's unconscious body—"to myself. If you do, I'll release your boyfriend. You have my word." He raised his hand, gold power streaming from it. "I'll swear on my magic, if I must."

"You must," I said, staring at him. "But how will you transfer the bond? I don't even know how it formed! I don't know what kind of bond it is!"

"It's a mate bond," Eamon said impatiently. "Surely you figured that much out." My mouth hung open. "Now, now," he chided. "We're running out of time." Faolain stirred on the floor and moaned.

"Swear," I demanded. "On your magic."

Eamon held up his hand, which was still glowing gold. "I swear that after the bond with Eileen O'Donnell is transferred to me, I will release her, and release Charles Talbot—" he gave me a wicked glance "—who also happens to be my brother. So mote it be." The gold glow died.

"Now," he said, walking toward me, "hold out your hand." Mute, reeling from the revelations, I extended my hand. "What do you mean, Charles is your brother?" I asked faintly.

"Now, now," he said, shaking his finger, "I never get in lovers' quarrels." Eamon smirked. "He won't talk about you at all—and believe me, he was asked many, many questions."

"It's you," I whispered, staring Eamon. "You're the one trying to seize the throne."

"Yes," he agreed complacently. "And with time, you might even come to support me." He extended his hand. It glowed blue, this time. "Take my hand," he whispered. "This won't hurt." Slowly, I placed my hand in his.

A jolt ran through me. It felt like the fire back at McConnell Consultants—running through me, enveloping me. I bit my lip, determined not to scream, and tasted blood.

"Good," Eamon said, releasing my hand, breathing heavily. "It's done."

I glared at him. Faolain moaned again.

"You'd best move," Eamon said delicately. "He won't be happy if he wakes up and finds you here. As far as he knows, *you* broke the bond. I," he smirked, "his faithful servant, tried to prevent you from fleeing and failed. If I might suggest, my dear, you might show your Anna the text messages you got from an untraceable source ... it might save your job. And if I were you, I'd keep this bond with me secret."

I swallowed, staring at me. "Charles?" I asked, voice breaking.

"Yes, yes," he waved his hand dismissively. "I'll see him released. Remember, I swore on my magic." He reached out and touched my face, almost gently. I felt a sting of magic and swore. "Better go," he murmured.

"What did you do to my face?"

He smiled. "Better go," Eamon repeated. Faolain opened his eyes. I turned and ran.

The guard wasn't at the door. I ran outside, and the valet stood aside. I wasn't imaging the smile on his face as I pelted into the car and frantically started it. I roared off, making straight for the NVRA.

My phone buzzed. It was from the same unknown number. It was a picture of an open cell door, and Charles leaving. I pressed my hand to my mouth to hold back a sob.

My phone buzzed again. I checked it. It was Anna.

"Unless you tell me you're on your way back to the office, you're fired."

One-handed, I texted her back. "I'm on my way."

"Good. We just got a Sending from one of our spies. Charles was just released. No word on the rest of his team."

Horrified, I pressed my hand to my mouth. I'd negotiated for Charles's safety and freedom. I hadn't said anything about the rest of the team.

Frantically, I texted back to the unknown number. "What about the others? You have to let them go!"

There was no reply.

Shaking, horrified, I drove back to base, Sheldon and Joe chortling in the back seat the whole way.

I parked the car and slowly got out. Garrett and Anna were standing at the door, arms crossed. I walked across the parking lot, feeling as though I was heading to my execution.

"Let's go," Anna said, looking sad. We went to the War Room.

Anna sat heavily. "Why did you leave?"

I pulled out my cell phone and unlocked it, handing it to her. "Look at the texts," I said quietly.

Anna and Garrett read the texts silently. They looked at each other, then at me. I felt a tear wend its way down my cheek.

"I couldn't—" I choked. "I couldn't leave him."

Anna sighed. "This," she said disgustedly, "is why I wish we had fraternization rules, like the military."

"To be fair," Garrett said, leaning forward, "they don't outrank each other. They're in separate departments. There's no violation."

Anna groaned, leaning back. "So what happened?"

I told them about going to the embassy. "Faolain—he told me he'd let Charles go if I went with him. But I hit him with a chair. Then Eamon came in. He told me he was behind the instability in the Kingdom of Northern Sun, that he wanted the throne, and that he'd let Charles go because it didn't fit his plans to keep him there." I put my hand to my mouth. "I just assumed he meant the rest of the team, too." I felt another tear trickle down my cheek. "Also," I said, voice breaking, "Faolain told me Jenny's a spy."

Garrett pushed his chair back sharply. "What?" He snapped.

"He told me that Jenny was working with him." I swallowed, feeling another tear track down my cheek.

Anna and Garrett looked at each other. "Interesting," Anna said, voice neutral. "Well, you've done your duty in reporting to us. We'll take it from here." She leaned back and crossed her arms.

"Eileen," she said, voice neutral, "I'm not going to fire you. Not now. But you showed serious lapses in judgment by going to the embassy alone. I am going to write you up."

"I understand," I replied, heart heavy. "What does that mean?"

She shrugged. "Think of it as a counseling statement. If it happens again, you will be fired." Anna met my eyes directly.

"I understand," I said, feeling a little better.

"Also," she said, pointing at me, "I want you to break it off with Charles."

"What?" I squeaked.

"I can't order you to do this," Anna said heavily. "But I want you to think about what just happened here. You put yourself in serious danger because of something that happened to him. He may have been targeted because of your ... relationship ... with Faolain." She paused. "Just think about it," she advised me kindly.

Garrett stood. "I think that's everything," he said, exchanging a look with Anna.

"When will Charles be back?" I asked eagerly.

Garrett and Anna exchanged another look. "Eileen, he's not coming back, not yet," Anna said gently. "We just heard from him. He found out his team hadn't been released and refused to leave the boundary area. He's going to try to go back in and save them."

"What?" I squeaked.

Anna sighed. "They were held in a guardhouse on the boundary," she said, voice thoughtful. "It's not the most secure facility. If the fae were serious about keeping the team captive, they'd have taken the team to the castle keep." She tapped her pen on the table. "He might have a chance."

I nodded, shaken. "He might," I echoed. I'd stopped praying after my head injury. I was too angry—at God, at everyone. I bowed my head and sent a prayer up for Charles's safety anyway, hoping He would hear me.

"Go home," Anna said tiredly. "Come in tomorrow, nine o'clock. We'll have more updates then." She waved her hand to the door. I nodded, grabbed my phone, and beat a hasty retreat.

I unlocked my car and got in, weeping freely now. It was too much. I couldn't handle it.

"No," a voice said from next to me. "You can't handle it." I jerked and looked over. Eamon sat next to me, smiling mysteriously. "Not without help," he continued.

"What are you doing here?" I asked angrily. "I took my medicine! I shouldn't be having hallucinations!"

"My dear," he said, still smiling, "I'm no hallucination. Unlike Faolain, I can actually use the bond the way it's intended. I'm speaking directly to you—to your mind." He paused. "In actuality," he confessed, "I'm in the middle of a very boring palace meeting, where the palace guard is being heavily ... chastised ... for allowing you to escape. All to the good. It'll just turn them against Faolain even more."

I gripped the steering wheel. "What do you mean?" I asked, voice breaking.

"A prince of the Kingdom of Northern Sun, defeated by a mere human? Not once, but twice?" Eamon snorted. "It hardly bears thinking about. Especially since the second time, he was taken down in his own bedroom. With a chair."

I gave a snort of laughter.

"That's more like it," Eamon said with approval. "My brother is a fool."

"Faolain? Yes, he is."

"Faolain, too," he said enigmatically. "But for now, my dear—go home. Sleep. Take your medicine. You'll feel better tomorrow." He disappeared.

I gripped the steering wheel tighter. Either my schizophrenia was getting worse, or Eamon really had just talked to me, mind-to-mind.

Chances are your schizophrenia is just getting worse, Joe said in my head.

Agreed, Sheldon added.

I punched the steering wheel, accidentally setting off the horn. "The fact that I'm not seeing you, just hearing you," I growled, "is a sign that my medication is working." The voices were silent.

I pulled out of the parking lot and turned the radio on high. I put it on the pop channel, singing aloud—defiantly, angrily—to each song.

Charles would come back. That was all that mattered. I frowned, thinking of Anna's advice. There were so many reasons this wouldn't work. Maybe it was better to give up. I bowed my head, feeling the tears start again.

"How could he not have told me he was Faolain's and Eamon's brother?" I whispered to myself, clutching the steering wheel. "How could he have done that?"

There were so many reasons this wouldn't work. Charles's secrets. My illness. My brain damage. Anna and Garrett's advice. Hopelessly, I pulled out my cell phone and stared at the picture of Charles in a cell, nearly swerving into the next lane. In the photo, Charles's face was bruised, one arm clearly broken. He lay as though dead.

"But he's free, now," I said fiercely. "He's free."

Not once they catch him freeing his teammates, Sheldon pointed out.

Whom you failed to free yourself, Joe snickered.

My phone rang. I started, then picked it up. "Hello?" I asked, trying to keep my voice from trembling.

"Eileen?"

"Who is this?" I shifted my phone to the other hand.

"Eileen, this—this is Sarah." The voice on the other end of the line took a deep breath. "You rescued me?"

I blinked. "Sarah? Are you all right?"

She didn't answer. "Come to the Unity Shelter," she said, voice almost robotic. "I need to see you."

"Sarah? Are you all right?"

"Just come!" A sob burst from her, and she hung up.

Frowning, I crossed three lanes of traffic to turn left. Car horns blared. "Oh, shut up," I muttered. I grabbed my pistol from where I'd stashed it under the seat and slid it over my shoulder. It hung there, a comforting weight.

I stopped at the Unity Shelter driveway. It was deserted. I stepped out of the car, pistol in my hand, and looked around. Something didn't feel right.

There was no access to the back of the house—it was surrounded by a fence. There was, however, a side door. I walked over to it and looked at the security system. The keypad flashed green. Praying they hadn't changed the passcode since I'd been there, I entered the number and held my breath. With a click, the door unlocked.

I slipped inside, pistol at the ready. The hallway was dark. A faint sound of crying drifted down the hall. I pressed my back against the wall, pointing my pistol in that direction. Slowly inching down the wall, I advanced.

The crying sounded like it was coming from the office. I crouched when I reached the intersection, pointing my pistol first down one hall, then the other. It was clear. I scuttled across the hall to right outside the office door. I pressed myself to the wall and, with a deep breath, pistol at the ready, I swung around and kicked the door in.

"Freeze," I snapped. Sarah was sitting in one of the chairs, sobbing. There was no one else there. "Sarah," I whispered, lowering my pistol, "What's going on? Where's Tara?"

"No, don't!" Sarah screamed, whipping around. "It's a trap, Eileen! It's a trap!"

Too late, I heard the door I'd smashed open close deliberately. "You're going to need a new lock," a woman's voice said with amusement.

I turned around, pistol back up. "I'll take that," the voice murmured, and the pistol sailed out of my grasp and into her hand.

I took a good long look. The woman was short and stocky, with long black hair and shocking blue eyes. I frowned. "Are you—"

"Fae? No. I'm half-and-half. Daddy kept me on to hunt down slaves. And now," she pointed at me, "he's asked me to hunt down you."

"What's your name?" I asked, stalling for time.

"Oh, do forgive me." She gave me a slight bow. "Adaline de Burgh, at your service." She smiled mockingly. "Though I really do think you might be at mine."

"You're from Western Wind."

"Yes," she nodded, unsurprised. "You met my sister, Severine. She always did have a soft spot for Charles Talbot. She was punished quite harshly when she returned without you."

"What do you want with me?" I asked, inching

my hand back to my pocket. She noticed.

"Don't think of trying to call for help," Adaline said mildly. "You're quite alone. As for what I want with you—what do you think? That we'd just let someone with a bond to Prince Faolain walk around?" She laughed.

"What did you do with Arianna and the others?" I asked angrily.

"Oh, they're around," she said, gesturing vaguely. "Sleep spell. Quite useful. And I think our intel about you having no magic is quite correct." Adaline eyed me curiously. "If you had magic, even the slightest amount, you'd have used it already. We read your personnel evaluations from the military, Eileen. Quite a change in performance over the years."

"I know I sucked," I said angrily, thinking desperately. What else could I do?

CHAPTER 9

"ARE YOU IN need of help?" a familiar voice drawled. I turned my head. Eamon stood there, shining gold.

"Don't speak," he said quickly. "You haven't mastered mind-to-mind yet, and we don't want any indication that you're talking to me." He paused. "I anticipated this, but you've acted so intelligently up until now. I never thought you'd do something so stupid." He frowned severely.

"What are you staring at?" Adaline's voice broke in. She squinted suspiciously at the space I was staring at.

"Nothing," I said. "Trying to plot my way free."

Adaline laughed. "You," she said. "I like you. Just because I do, I won't take Sarah here back to Northern Sun." She smiled. "Consider it an even trade."

"And where are we going?" I asked, stalling for time.

"We, Eileen, are going to Western Wind. You'll be an honored guest. Until Prince Faolain irritates the Powers That Be too much, and then—" she drew her hand across her throat. I swallowed.

"Where's Tara?"

"Well. I told Sarah that I had her in the car, ready to go back to Northern Sun—or kill her—if her mother didn't cooperate." Adaline's lips lifted in a dry smile. "In actuality, Tara is asleep. I don't kill babies." She pointed the pistol at me. "I do, however, shoot valuable hostages in non-essential parts of their bodies to convince them to move."

I raised my hands and slowly moved toward her. I calculated the distance between her and me. If I could just get close enough ... but before I got within an arm's reach, Adaline stopped me.

"There you go," she said. "I know you throw a good punch. I won't have you knocking me out." She laughed and, pistol still pointed at me, circled so she was standing behind me. I sighed. I'd hoped she would turn her back for a second. Slowly, I moved to the door. Sarah still sobbed behind me.

"Sarah," I called, "it's okay. Don't worry."

She didn't answer, just sobbed even harder.

"Let's go." Adaline prodded my back with the pistol.

Charles would never let me live this down. If I ever got to see him again. Bleakly, I allowed her to push and prod me closer to the door.

"Faster," Adaline warned, "or I'll put a bullet in you and carry you out myself." Sighing, I picked up the pace a little, but still moved deliberately slowly.

There was a shot, and a blaze of heat crossed my thigh. Sarah and I both screamed. I clutched my leg, feeling the blood welling out.

"That was just a graze," Adaline said, sounding impatient. "But I'm dead serious. There won't be another warning. Pick up the pace."

I picked up the pace. There was no one at the front door. I looked around, dismayed that Eamon wasn't there to help me. Adaline guided me back to my car. "Keys," she said, holding out her hand. I placed my keys in her hand. Still keeping me at gunpoint, she unlocked the driver's side and pointed at it. "Get in."

Obediently, I slid into the front seat. Adaline kept the keys as she walked around to the passenger's door, opened it, and slid in. She handed me the keys and pointed the gun at me. "Drive."

"Where?" I asked, pulling out.

"I'll give you directions." She leaned back, gun still pointed at me. "Take a right."

I took the right and glanced at my rearview mirror. I recognized that green car. I glanced sideways at Adaline, wondering if she realized we had a tail.

"Keep driving."

Apparently not. She hadn't glanced at the mirrors once. *Charles would call her an amateur*, I thought. I turned the wheel sharply to the right. The green car followed.

"Wha—" Adaline caught herself. "What are you doing? I told you to keep driving!"

"And I am," I pointed out. "You never said what direction." I smirked. "What are you going to do? Shoot the driver? We'll crash and both die if that happens, and you know it."

"Turn around." Adaline waved the pistol threateningly at me.

"No." I kept driving. I was headed for one spot that I knew very well.

"Turn around!"

I sped up. The car behind me sped up as well, matching my speed. Adaline blanched. I knew she'd caught sight of the green car. She aimed the gun at my head. "I will kill you," she threatened.

"Good luck driving the car without me!" I laughed. "At this speed, we'll crash. The passenger's side doesn't have an airbag—sorry."

My destination was in sight—the police station. I fishtailed into the parking lot. Startled officers ran out of the station. Adaline shot the pistol at me. I ducked, and the shot went through the window. The police officers surrounded the car, pointing their weapons at it. "Get out of the car!" one shouted.

I raised my hands and pointed at Adaline. "She has a gun pointed at me!" I screamed.

"And I will shoot!" Adaline shouted. The pistol was wobbling as she tried to figure out what to do. "Don't doubt it!"

"Ma'am." One officer tried to reason with her. "If you shoot her, we shoot you. Do you really want it to end that way?"

"I'm dead anyway," Adaline snapped. "The Kingdom of Western Wind doesn't forgive mistakes."

"If we arrest you here," the officer pointed out, "you're arrested on human territory. You go to a human jail."

Adaline's eyes wavered. "I want protection," she said grimly. "They won't give up."

The officer smiled calmly. "I think we can make that work," he said.

"All right. All right." Adaline slowly lowered the pistol. "I'm coming out." She pulled on the handle of the passenger door, levering herself out.

Suddenly, she began to choke. Her hands went to her throat, and her eyes bulged with terror. Saliva dripped from her mouth as she struggled to scream.

"Get a bus!" The officer who'd been talking to her ran to her side. "It's some kind of poison," he said distractedly. He pulled a small dart from her neck and rolled her onto her side. Another officer knelt next to him. "Get her inside," he said distractedly, waving at me. I stepped out of the car, hands still in the air. Two officers grabbed me and hustled me into the station. As we went, I looked over my shoulder; the green car rolled slowly by. The driver lifted his hand in a laconic wave.

"Is there anyone we should call?" one of the officers, a young woman, asked. I shivered. "My phone—it's still in the car. I need to call my mother—

my brother—my boss—" The woman looked down and spotted the blood on my leg. It had stopped bleeding, but there was a blood trail down my pants.

She smiled sympathetically. "It'd be a really bad time to go back out to your car, ma'am. Why don't you come in here and we can get you something to drink, and something to bandage up your leg. Do you want to go to the hospital?" She led me to a small lounge off to the side. I looked around. A utilitarian blue sofa sat next to a microwave. A circular table with hard-looking chairs occupied the middle of the room.

"No! No hospital," I said. I looked at the table. "It's the Knights of the Round Table," I giggled, pointing.

The officer looked at me with confusion. "Ma'am?"

"Nothing," I said, still giggling. "I think I'm having a nervous breakdown." I laughed harder, sitting down on the couch and putting my head in my hands.

"Ma'am, how about some water?" I felt a hand nudge my shoulder and looked up, feeling my eyes fill with tears. The officer was standing there with a bottle, looking concerned. In her other hand she held an ace bandage and gauze. "I think this'll be wide enough to wrap the bullet graze," she added. "Though you have to promise me you'll go to the doctor when your ride gets here."

"Thanks," I choked out, grabbing the bottle and downing half of it. "I appreciate it. I promise I will."

I began to wrap my leg with the ace bandage, plac-
ing the gauze over the small wound.

"Of course," she said, sitting down next to me.
"My name's Maria. What's your name?"

"Eileen," I said. I drank more of the water and
went back to binding my wound. "Eileen O'Donnell."

"Well, Eileen—may I call you that?" I nodded.
"It's a pleasure to meet you. You were very brave back
there," she said, watching my face closely. "Can I ask
what happened?"

I took a deep breath and told her part of the
story. I told her how I'd saved Sarah and taken her
to the Unity Shelter; how I'd gotten a strange call
and gone over; how Adaline had been there, waiting.
Maria frowned, nodding.

"Why was she there?" she asked. "What did
she want?"

I sighed. I didn't want to tell this part of the story.
"I don't know," I said awkwardly. "She just threatened
me with a pistol and asked me to come. I didn't ask
for the details."

Maria frowned again, her eyes searching my
face. "That's very strange," she said slowly. I nodded
and shrugged. "I guess, yeah. I mean, she's fae. Who
knows why they do anything?"

Maria looked at me but said nothing. I looked back.

"She doesn't believe you," Eamon observed. He
appeared at my side, glowing gold. "You're a terrible
liar, my dear."

I opened my mouth and closed it. "Maria," I said instead, "I left my medication in my car. Is there any way I can get that? And my phone?"

Maria sighed. "Let me go check on that," she said. "Wait here." She got up and left. I heard her footsteps echo down the hall. As soon as they were out of earshot, I swung to Eamon and cursed at him.

"Oh my," Eamon said, eyeing me speculatively. "Spicy." He smirked. "Faolain would never have appreciated you."

"I have no idea what you're talking about," I said, voice cold. Eamon smiled at me.

"Eileen," he said, voice soft, "I just want you to consider this. When you had your ... accident ..." he looked at me, head tilted, "your prefrontal cortex was damaged. That happens to the fae, as well. Look up the legend of King Phillip, of Western Wind." Eamon snapped his fingers. "And with that little bit of wisdom," he waved his hands dramatically, "I am gone." He vanished.

I growled in annoyance and leaned back in the chair. I could feel a headache coming on.

"Eileen?" Maria appeared back at the door. "I have your phone and your purse. I hope your medicine is there—I checked around the car and couldn't find it." She held both out.

"Yes, thank you," I said gratefully. I dug around my purse until I found my emergency migraine medication. "I just need this," I explained. "I'm getting a ferocious migraine."

"Perfectly understandable," Maria murmured, her face carefully blank. I swallowed the medicine and took another sip of water. "How long do I need to stay?" I asked. "I'd like to go home. Migraine medication always makes me sleepy."

"You're free to go, Eileen," Maria said, "but unfortunately we have to keep your car. It's a crime scene."

I nodded. "I understand. I'll call my brother."

Fortunately, Nate picked up on the first ring. "Eileen," he said, sounding genuinely frightened, "Where are you? What's going on?"

Wearily, I rubbed at my forehead. "Nate, can you come pick me up from the police station? I'm at the one in Woodbridge."

"The police station," he repeated, sounding stunned. "Sure. Are you under arrest or something? Do you need a lawyer?

"No, no," I said hastily, "nothing like that." I snuck a glance at Maria, who was still studying me. "I just— need a ride home. I'll explain when you get here."

"All right," he said slowly, "no problem. I'm getting in my car now." He hung up. I lowered my phone and sighed. "Do you mind if I take a nap?" I asked Maria. "I'll just stretch out here on the sofa.

"Absolutely," Maria said, her face breaking out into a smile. "I'll wake you up when your brother gets here.

I laid on the sofa and resolutely shut my eyes. The migraine medication usually sent me to sleep; I could feel it tugging at the corners of my eyes, tempting me to descend. There was nothing I wanted to do more. But I couldn't stop thinking of Charles. Where was he? What was he doing? Was he all right?

I must've fallen asleep, because I dreamed the most vivid dream. I was standing in a forest clearing, next to Charles. Charles was lying on his stomach, with binoculars trained on something far away. An orb of blue fire surrounded him. I blinked, and then knelt.

"Charles?" I asked tentatively. He didn't look up. "Charles!" With that, he lowered his binoculars, frowning.

"What—"

"Charles!" I put my hand on the blue fire orb, and immediately felt a sharp shock of pain. I looked down and saw my flesh redden.

I sat up on the sofa, breathing heavily, feeling disoriented. My hand still hurt. I curled my fingers around it automatically, and then frowned. I opened my hand and looked at it. The flesh was reddened, as though it'd been burned.

"Eileen?" Maria walked in and caught me staring at my hand. She walked over, frowning. "What a terrible burn! Did that happen when you were in the car?"

"It must have," I whispered, closing my fingers over it again. "Everything is so blurry."

"Of course," Maria said sympathetically. "I just wanted to let you know—your brother is here."

"Oh! Nate's here?" I frowned. "That was really fast."

She smiled gently. "You've been asleep for almost an hour, Eileen."

I blinked. "The medicine really puts me out," I said with an uneasy laugh. "Thank you for letting me know, Maria. I truly appreciate it."

"Absolutely." Maria hesitated. "Just one last thing," she said quietly. "If you ever decide to tell the truth about why that fae was after you—just know that I'm willing to listen to you."

I stared, slightly stunned. "Thank you," I whispered, "but I really can't tell any more than I already have."

"I understand," Maria said, putting her hand on my arm. I twitched. She noticed and released my arm. "Here, let me give you my card." She pulled out her wallet and produced a business card. "Officer Maria Sanchez," it read. Nothing else was on the card except for a phone number.

"Thank you," I repeated, staring at the card. It seemed odd that it wouldn't have a department on it.

"Not a problem at all," Maria said. "Why don't I walk you out to your brother?"

Nate was sitting at a police officer's desk. The building was almost empty—it looked like the entire force had adjourned outside to examine my car. I shuddered at the thought of the insurance premium

I was sure to be charged. For a moment, I wondered how you would report "pistol shots from crazed fae assassin" and then dismissed it from my mind.

"Be careful," Eamon's voice whispered. I looked up to see him there, floating, surrounded by gold fire once more, looking at me gravely. "Faolain isn't playing the game much right now—his face creased in a wicked smile—"but remember, he's not the only one in town. You're safe from me, my dear. You are not safe from Western Wind."

I gave a shallow nod. Eamon smiled sharply. "Excellent," he said. "This'll be an interesting game. You don't play it well, but at least you're quick on your feet." He disappeared again.

I walked up to Nate and tried to smile. "Ready to go?" I asked.

Nate stared at me and exploded from his chair, almost knocking it over. "You've got to be kidding," he burst out. "First something crazy goes down at your work—you still haven't told me or Mom why you didn't come home last night—and now I'm picking you up from a police station? What's going on?"

I sighed. "I'll explain in the car," I promised, walking to the door. Before I opened it, I hesitated and turned around to look at Maria again. "Adaline," I said, with some difficulty. "Did she survive?"

"Yes," Maria said gently. "She did." She paused. "She's in a coma now, but she is expected to live." Maria looked at me very levelly. "The poison used seems to have originated in the Northern Wild—but you didn't hear that from me."

I nodded, feeling tired. I had so many questions. Why had Eamon insisted on transferring the bond to himself? Surely there was another way to handle it. Who had shot the dart? Who had supplied the poison? Who had sent Will, the unknown operative, to my Muay Thai class? And—I froze, remembering the very beginning of my saga—who had sent the first Sending, warning me to run?

I smiled politely at Maria. "I have no idea what you just said," I replied. Maria nodded back, smirking slightly.

"Let's go," Nate said, grabbing his keys. "You look like you're about to fall over." Together, we walked to the parking lot.

"So, what happened?" Nate asked, as we got into the car. I sighed. "Stupidity," I said disgustedly. I should never have gone into the shelter without calling for backup first. Briefly, I wondered what I had been thinking, then sighed. I hadn't been. I was a trained, former army lieutenant—I had no excuse.

I told Nate what had happened as we drove. He was mostly silent, every now and then interjecting a "what!" or a "wow."

"Mom's going to be pissed, isn't she," I said at the end of my recitation.

Nate glanced at me out of the corner of his eye. "Probably. You were pretty stupid."

"Hey!"

"Well, you were," he said. "What were you thinking, running into the shelter with no backup?" His eyes narrowed. "And you never did say why you didn't come home last night."

"Just a really bad migraine," I lied. "I had to sleep at the NVRA because I didn't want to drive."

"I don't mind picking you up." Nate's eyes were still narrowed suspiciously.

"I know, Nate," I said heavily. "But I don't like treating you as my personal chauffeur." He looked at me, and I relented. "There was some operation-related drama going down," I told him.

"What do you mean?"

I suppressed a sigh. I could tell Nate would be a good lawyer—he never let anything go. He was worse than a dog with a bone.

"Charles was captured," I admitted, "along with his team."

Nate's eyes flew open. "What?" he asked, horrified.

"I don't know where he is now," I said, eyes clouding with tears.

"Oh, Eileen." Nate gently touched my shoulder. "I'm so sorry."

I nodded, covering my mouth with my hand. The burn tingled, and I flinched.

"What's wrong?" Nate asked, worried.

"It's ... it's a burn," I murmured, holding it out. It seemed to get pinker as I looked at it.

"It most definitely is!" Nate said, shocked. "Did that happen when you were in the car with the fae kidnapper?"

"Adaline," I corrected absently. "And yes, it must have."

He grabbed my hand and looked carefully at it. "Lady of the Lake, Eileen. I think you need to go to urgent care. This is a nasty burn."

I took a longer look at it. It was deep, but the last thing I wanted to do was stay out. I wanted to curl up in my bed, in my pajamas, with a cup of hot tea.

"Later," I said absently.

"No, now," Nate said, twisting the steering wheel. "It'll scar and you might lose function in the hand."

I laughed. "Where did you learn that, biology class?"

"*Forensic Magic*," he corrected me. We drove for about ten more minutes in silence. I was falling asleep when we pulled into urgent care.

"Go ahead," he urged me. "Go in. I'll just sit out here and read." He retrieved a thick tome from the back of the car.

"*An Analysis of Marbury v Madison*?" I asked as I got out. "You must be really bored." He grunted, already immersed in his text.

I walked into urgent care and up to patient registration. The medical assistant looked up. "Hi," I said politely. "I need my hand looked at. And my leg." I held my hand up for her inspection, then pointed at my leg.

She raised her eyebrows. "Nasty burn," she observed. She pushed the magi-pad over to me. It sparked blue.

I sighed. "I can't use magic," I told her. She raised her eyebrows again but gestured for me to sit down. "Don't worry," she said, "I'll fill it in for you." A thin trail of fire extended from her finger. "Put your hand up to mine," she instructed. I placed my palm against hers and smiled at the cool feeling. She transferred my palm to the pad, smiling in satisfaction.

"All done," she said, pulling the pad back. "You'll be called in the order you came in." I nodded and headed into the waiting room. "Thank you," I called over my shoulder. She waved her hand in acknowledgement.

I sat down and pulled out my phone with a sigh. I should text Anna and let her know what happened. I blinked when I saw I had four missed calls, all from—Charles? I hit "call back" and held the phone up to my ear. He answered on the first ring.

"Hey, babe," he said breezily. I frowned in surprise. He'd never called me that before. "Where are you?"

"I'm ... at urgent care," I said slowly. "Charles, how are you?"

"I'm good! I'm good." He paused. "Can I see you?"

"Of course," I said, still surprised. He hadn't asked me what was wrong, which was very unlike him.

"Which urgent care are you at?"

"The one in Woodbridge," I said, giving him the address. "See you soon?"

"Absolutely, babe." He hung up the phone. I put mine away distractedly. Soon I would see Charles again. My heart filled with joy. That dream of him being out in the woods, peering through binoculars and surrounded by an orb of blue fire, was just that—a dream. I looked at my hand, frowning, and then dismissed it. Doubtless it had happened during the car chase.

Just then, the doors swung open and Charles walked in. He looked around the waiting room before spotting me and sauntering over. I watched him move, feeling a little on edge. He moved like a hunter. My spine twinged with energy. It felt like something wasn't right.

Then Charles smiled at me, and all that was forgotten. "Hey, babe," he greeted me, pulling me up and kissing me. I stiffened. Maybe it was everything I had been through that day, but it felt wrong. He felt me stiffen and immediately released me. "Babe," he said, sounding hurt, "what's wrong?"

I swallowed. "Nothing," I murmured, sticking out my hand. "I'm just—I thought you were still in the boundary area, searching for your team!"

Charles stared at my hand for a moment, then reached out and gently gripped it. "Not to worry, babe," he said, smiling at me gently. "I always come back." I nodded slowly.

"So sit down," he suggested. "Tell me about your day." He slid into a seat and patted the seat next to him in invitation. I slid down as well, sighing in exhaustion.

"Oh, Charles," I said. "I'm so exhausted." I felt tears well up in my eyes.

"I know, babe," he said comfortingly. He patted my shoulder. "Sounds like you had a long day, between Eamon and Faolain and then Adaline," he murmured.

I stiffened, then forced myself to relax. *He could've learned all that from Anna and Garrett*, I told myself.

But then, Sheldon pointed out, *you haven't told Anna about Adaline yet, have you?*

A memory surfaced: Garrett, lecturing me on proper protocol for entering the War Room. "Some of the fae can shape-shift. We had one shifter try to get into the War Room, but he was caught when he didn't know the passcode."

Some of the fae can shape-shift ...

I straightened slightly. "Charles," I said casually, "When we get out of here, can we go back to where we had our first date? Luigi's?"

"Absolutely, babe," Charles said casually. "You know how much I love Italian." He smiled at me. I smiled back, automatically.

"I'm just going to text my brother," I told him, pulling out my cell phone. "I've been waiting awhile and he might want to leave. Now that you're here, though, you can drive me." I smiled at him. He nodded, seriously.

"Absolutely, babe."

He watched my phone as I texted Nate. "Go ahead and leave. I'm good to go here."

A few moments later, my phone buzzed. "Are you sure?"

"Absolutely. I'm as good as fire is red," I texted. I swallowed, hoping he'd get the message, and lowered my phone to look innocently at not-Charles. Not-Charles smiled at me and stroked my face. "I'm so glad I'm back," he whispered. "I missed you." He leaned forward for a kiss, and I quickly turned my face away. The kiss caught me on the cheek instead. He frowned. I laughed, unsteadily.

"I'm sorry, Charles," I told him. "I'm just really tired." I yawned for dramatic effect. "Do you mind if I sleep on your shoulder?"

"Of course not, babe," he murmured, patting my shoulder comfortingly. "Go ahead."

"Thank you," I said brightly, leaning against him. I closed my eyes, feigning sleep.

"In trouble again?" Eamon's voice asked sarcastically. I cracked open my eyes to see him crouched down, his face barely an inch from mine. "You're lucky I'm resourceful."

I hissed through my teeth at him.

"Oh, you're resourceful too," Eamon conceded.

"That little gambit with your brother was a good one. I take it that was code of some type? Red for enemy? Hopefully he gets it." Eamon leaned back a little, looking at me speculatively. "Last time," he murmured, "you managed to save yourself, without my help. You have no idea how badly that wounds my pride." He smirked. "Now this—you're just a magnet for trouble, aren't you?" He tsked at me, then vanished.

Not-Charles touched my shoulder. "Hey babe," he said. "They're ready for you." He paused. "Want me to come back with you?" The medical assistant was standing next to him, looking sympathetic.

"No, no," I said, "Don't worry about me. You just stay and rest. I know how tired you must be." I smiled brightly at him.

"I really think I should come with you," not-Charles said, starting to stand.

"No, no," I said, pressing him down. "Please. I'd feel so guilty if I let you move." I stood next to the medical assistant. "Ready!" I chirped. She nodded, looking carefully at my eyes. We moved toward the door to the inner area of the clinic in silence.

"Ma'am," she said, "please sit here." She pointed to a booth with a blood pressure cuff and a scale. She shot me a troubled look and got out the blood pressure cuff. When she leaned over to put it on my arm, she whispered to me.

"Ma'am, are you safe right now?"

"No," I whispered back urgently. "I need to get out of here."

She gave me a slight nod and finished taking my blood pressure. "I'll go get the doctor," she said. She gave me a significant look. I nodded, trembling slightly. She left, but I saw her lift the telephone and make a call at one of the stations.

Less than a minute later, she came in with the doctor. "Well, well, Ms. O'Donnell," the doctor boomed jovially. "I'm Dr. Hatsuka. Let's take a look at your leg and arm." As he unwrapped my leg, he cast me a long look from under his lashes. "Security is en route," he told me quietly.

"Thank you," I mouthed, leaning back and closing my eyes. He examined my leg in silence and then turned to the medical assistant. "Go get me a burn pack," he told her, "and a fresh bandage." He turned back to me. "Should only be a few more moments."

"Should it?"

I looked up to see not-Charles standing outside my booth, smiling easily. I froze in horror. Beside me, I saw the doctor freeze as well. "One of the other medical assistants let me back," he explained casually. "I just wanted to be with you, babe." He crossed his arms and leaned on the wall, smiling at me.

I started to shake. "Get out," I hissed.

"What?" He straightened up, looking genuinely surprised.

"Get out!" I snapped. "You're not Charles. Get out!"

Not-Charles turned to the doctor. "Please, doctor," he said earnestly, "I'm her boyfriend. She's schizophrenic, and I'm afraid she's having a breakdown."

The doctor studied him for a moment. "I'll evaluate her," he said after a moment, "but I'm afraid you'll have to leave, sir. She doesn't want you here, and she's entitled to that."

Not-Charles seemed to grow bigger. "What?" he asked, voice ugly.

"You heard me," the doctor repeated, not budging. Behind not-Charles, I saw the medical assistant coming back, hands full of bandages and the burn pack. She saw not-Charles and halted in surprise. I caught her eye. Run, I mouthed. She dropped the bandages and backed up, eyes on not-Charles.

Fortunately, he didn't seem to notice. His eyes were on the doctor. "No one says no to me." He grabbed the doctor around the throat and lifted, growing even larger. I screamed and hurled myself at him, trying to get him to release the doctor. Not-Charles batted me back with a single hand. I threw my wrist up to protect my face and crashed into the wall. I felt my wrist break.

Now that was a mistake, I thought muzzily. *I know how to fall.* I edged my way up the wall, trying not to lose my balance. I felt dizzy.

Not-Charles dropped the doctor with a snarl.

I rushed him again, trying to get the doctor away from him; not-Charles grabbed me, lips twisted in a vicious snarl. I gagged. His breath smelled like raw meat.

"I was promised meat," he said in a deep growl, "for bringing you home." He lifted me by the throat, just as he had the doctor. I thrashed, trying to scream. I heard a commotion but couldn't see what it was, I was totally focused on not-Charles.

"Drop her!" A voice yelled. Was that Anna? Not-Charles looked over his shoulder and, with a sneer, released his hand. I fell to the ground, retching. Not-Charles put his hands up.

"I surrender," he growled. "I invoke the Fae-Human Treaty of 1785—" he swayed, his hands going to his throat. I watched, dazed, as he fell to the ground, blood spurting from his neck.

"Jenny!" It was Anna's voice again. "Why did you shoot him? We could've gotten valuable intel from him!"

"I thought he had something in his hand," Jenny said stubbornly. "Don't you see? He does!"

"So he does," Garrett's voice rumbled. "But we can check it out later. Right now, let's take care of Eileen and the doctor." I felt a presence kneel at my side. "Clever, using that code to text your brother," he told me, as he gently felt along my head. "He called us and told us you were in trouble."

I gasped. "Dr. Hatsuka—the medical assistant—"

"The medical assistant is fine." I felt his hands pause. "Dr. Hatsuka is dead," he said softly. "I'm sorry, Eileen."

I felt tears well up in my eyes. Behind him, I saw Eamon floating, regarding me carefully. He flickered out as sight as soon as I saw him.

"Who was he?" I gestured at the body of not-Charles.

"I don't know," Garrett said heavily. "Most of the shifters come from the Northern Wild. We usually don't get them down here." He paused for a moment and then carefully touched my forehead. "I can't heal your wrist, or completely heal your concussion," he told me, "but I can make them a bit better. Would that be all right?"

I nodded, squinting my eyes against the brightness of the fire in his hand. Without another word, Garrett placed his hand on my chest. I sighed in relief as I felt the pain ease.

"Charles?" I asked eagerly.

Garrett paused for a moment, then shook his head. "Still no word," he said softly. He helped me sit up.

I rubbed my eyes and looked over at not-Charles's body. In death, he seemed to have reverted to his original form. He was gorilla-shaped, with dark red streaks around his mouth—they looked crusted on, I noted in horror, like blood. I looked at Garrett.

"Is that—"

"Blood? Almost certainly." Garrett leaned back on his heels and examined the body with a clinical eye. "Nasty creature."

I shuddered. "Nate didn't come back with you, did he?" I asked. Surely he wouldn't be that foolish.

"He wanted to," Garrett told me, "But we made him wait at base." He smiled. "He took that about as well as you would have."

I swallowed and nodded. "There are so many questions," I whispered.

Garrett nodded. "And not enough answers," he said cheerfully. "That's all right. That's why we're here." He extended a hand and pulled me gently to my feet.

"Take tomorrow off," he instructed me, "but I want to see you back at work, bright and early, the day after." He smiled and tipped me a salute before heading off to where Anna was talking to the medical assistant.

I leaned back, covering my face. So many questions. Not enough answers. I thought briefly of Charles, somewhere in the boundary lands ... and poor Dr. Hatsuka. I raised my chin, determined.

It was time to fight.

...to be continued in
Kingdom of the Western Wind

Made in the USA
Monee, IL
18 September 2019